PRETERNATURAL

BOOK 1

Welcome to Meadowsville...

PETER TOPSIDE

Preternatural, Revised Edition

Copyright © 2022 Peter Topside

Published by Meadowsville Quill, LLC

Paperback ISBN: 978-1-7363472-4-9
Hardcover ISBN: 978-1-7363472-5-6
eISBN: 978-1-7363472-6-3

Cover and Interior Design: GKS Creative
Project Management: The Cadence Group
Editing: Monti Shalosky

This is a work of fiction that contains graphic violence, strong language, and psychologically distressing elements.

I dedicate this book, and the odd number of chapters, to my adoring wife. She always encourages me to embrace the unevenness in life.

Contents

Preface

I first want to thank all of my readers for taking the journey
into my twisted, fantastical little world. I spent more than
twenty-five years devising this trilogy, going through
countless concepts and drafts, before settling on what you are
about to read.

I grew up in a very abusive situation and used writing as
my outlet for all of my anger, processing the various traumas
that I endured, and made it a strongpoint. In a lot of ways,
it was very therapeutic and mirrors my own journey toward
better mental health, which I remain a strong advocate of. But
I am not a trained or formally educated writer and have no
previous experience in the literary world. So while my stories
may not be of the same caliber of some of my better-known
colleagues, I am extremely proud of each book and the tire-
less work that I put in to make a lifelong goal happen, not just

once but three times. And I am so humbled and grateful for the encouragement and support from my friends, family, fellow authors and readers, and the professional help that I had to make it all happen.

All of the characters and situations described in these books are all based on parts of myself and things I either was directly subjected to or witnessed firsthand. I took some liberties to keep things more theatrical and entertaining, but all events in the book have a reason for being there and some basis in reality. To me, direct experiences allowed me to accurately depict how each character would react and feel and how to navigate the story as a whole.

The books were written to be very layered, in that someone could read it surface-level and appreciate as just another horror story. However, I incorporated many psychological principles and tons of symbolism throughout that will all give my readers something to dive into and really analyze, if they want to take it to that level. One of the most important things when I wrote this trilogy was to allow each reader to have their own unique experience.

And, of course, at its core, I wanted to develop one helluva horror story. I am a self-described "horror junkie" and have more hours clocked in on horror movies, scary books, and other such outlets than I care to admit. But horror is something that I was raised with, bred alongside, and had to deal with, so it feels like home to me. While I respect other authors and their works in alternative genres, I think horror is the place that I not only started writing in but will continue in, until the day I finally put my little idea pad and special four-color writing pen down for good.

Anyway, without further introduction, please enjoy your stay in Meadowsville . . .

1

Meadowsville

Inside a pristine Meadowsville council chambers, the visibly riled crowd overrode Mayor Valerie Wilkins. The pure white walls and freshly polished pews brightened the room but were stifled by an overly darkened maroon rug and the ugly mood of the townspeople.

"Order, order," Mayor Wilkins attempted to bark over the crowd, but to no avail.

A substantial police presence stood at the front of the meeting, almost completely surrounding the township administration—consisting of Police Chief Rupert Jones, Mayor Wilkins, and both the township administrator and chief financial officer. Each of the officers wore a light sheen of sweat as the commotion from the crowd intensified. The room was full of a thick, stagnant air from the all the volatility.

Mayor Wilkins stood tall at the podium, looking over everyone with a stern expression, not wavering in her stance to the outcry of her citizens. Her expensive navy blue power suit and stoic demeanor exemplified her resolve and steadiness. She absorbed the yelling and insults as she had done many times before. And she never allowed it to bother her in the least. This was her town, and she had the ultimate say on how things were run, whether anyone liked it or not.

"This John Smith crap is out of control," one of the audience members yelled out. "Have you seen all the graffiti in the high school and on Highway 6?"

Mayor Wilkins finally put her hand up to silence the rumblings of everyone so she could respond, but more shouts overpowered her efforts.

"What are you doing to stop it?" someone else called out.

"How are you people protecting our families?" a haggard looking middle-aged man barked.

"I understand your concerns and feel your frustrations—" Wilkins began in a calm, yet assertive tone.

"How could you? You don't even live in town!" someone else interjected.

"Hey, shut up and let 'er talk," one of the mayor's supporters demanded.

"Please give me a chance to speak. I understand where you're coming from. And I see the areas we can improve," she said.

The crowd overwhelmed her again, and she stammered a few times before raising her voice to take charge of the group, "Please! We're not solving anything by talking over each other!

If you all can't control yourselves, you'll be escorted out. Now, quiet down so we can start this meeting."

Some of the attendees began to quiet down, and Mayor Wilkins finally saw her opportunity to jump into business to get this meeting over as quickly as she could. Not that she actually cared about their concerns anyway. Everything was going according to plan. The crowd couldn't stop anything. Their efforts were no more meaningful than a bunch of gnats buzzing around her at this point, and she quietly tried to hide an arrogant smirk behind her stone-cold face.

"You all have copies of this year's proposed budget. As you can see, the increased tourism has generated a thirty percent growth in our already stellar profits over last year. I have approved a higher budget for both public works and the police department to ensure you all feel a satisfactory level of safety and efficiency in this community," she assured them.

"The cops don't do anything as it is. The gangs, missing people, all of it is out of hand. We've heard all this before, and nothing ever changes. And you want to pay them more," an older woman hollered.

"I've lived here for forty years and never had a problem," another man announced.

Police Chief Jones remained still and silent, in full uniform, not attempting to interject. He was well aware of the situation and limitations that his department worked under each and every day. But these meetings had been progressively worsening over the last few months. Having been on the force for over thirty years, witnessing the absurdities in Meadowsville had prematurely aged him in many ways. But this recent movement demanding change was growing stronger by the day. Mayor Wilkins was on borrowed time, and he just hoped to outlast her, preserving his position.

A cold sweat covered his forehead. He took out a handkerchief from his pocket and blotted the moisture, running the cloth back across his silver crew cut. A few loose beads made their way into the crow's feet surrounding his increasingly aged eyes.

"I assure you all that Meadowsville is very safe for you and your families. Our levels of incidents, despite its tremendous size, are statistically less than any other local area. I mean, we're about seventy-five thousand people over twenty miles. If you don't believe me, I'll direct you to Police Chief Jones." Mayor Wilkins motioned to him.

Chief Jones attempted to speak, but she cut him off. "And I assure you all that I promise to keep the taxes from going up again if you reelect me later this year. This would be a record third year in a row that I've accomplished this during my tenure as your mayor."

Jones's furrowed his brow in frustration, making the wrinkles on his forehead much more prominent.

"We don't want all these tourists here anymore. They're causing us more harm than good," another resident shouted.

"I don't know if I agree with that. I think we just need to control them better," a nearby gentleman squawked.

The room exploded in anger again as the residents, who either approved or disagreed with Mayor Wilkins's handling of the town, clashed. She bellowed over them, commanding their attention again. The tension in the air could be cut with a knife.

"As we ramp up police efforts, we will rightfully deal with any issues that outsiders bring into our beloved town. But please keep in mind that if we were to act too harshly and create further taxes, costs, or troubles for tourists, I will be unable to guarantee taxes not being raised. It would reduce how many people visit Meadowsville. And despite a few bad apples here and there, the tourists are very lucrative and beneficial for us to host. I don't want to change the course we've been on and don't think anyone would disagree with me on that either."

"What about John Smith and the gangs? And those hellhounds too" another resident challenged.

Mayor Wilkins took a deep breath, reminding herself to not say the name "Mr. Smith," as it would just bring more unnecessary attention to the obvious problem at hand. This monstrosity had been in the town since its inception and had brought tourists from around the country to see. It was talked about almost as much as a bigfoot or any other popular urban legend. She could not and would not allow anyone to jeopardize this tradition under her watch. It was far too profitable.

"People, it is my promise to you that we can do better, and we will do better. Any safety concerns will be continued to be managed by our administration," she said.

Someone laughed in the back of the crowd and hollered, "Thanks for the fake promises. I see how you all protected the little Evans boy and the Cohen family. Not even a police report got filed. Explain that, you arrogant bitch. You don't care about us. You only care about yourself."

Mayor Wilkins paused at the remark and looked at the large clock at the other side of the room, seeing the time at 9:00 p.m. A small crack in the top right corner illuminated the large hand over the twelve, acting like a figurative sign to end the meeting. She breathed a sigh of relief, knowing she had been saved by the curfew. This was the exact reason she held these meetings later in the evening, so it could always be a diversion tactic to utilize. The crowds spent so much time screaming that she could stall to run out the clock.

"As we express our concerns about public safety, it is my responsibility to enforce compliance to the curfew that we put in place. Please get home quickly and safely. This meeting is now adjourned. Thank you all for your time," she said passively and hastily, exiting with the township administration, followed by the police.

"Why don't you have open office hours anymore? You afraid you'll have to actually answer our questions and do your job?" another member of the town called to the mayor but was ignored.

The crowd began to dissemble, now speaking in smaller groups as they exited the building. A man who had quietly kept to himself in the back row was the last person to stand up. He wore a black and purple Meadowsville Market uniform with the name tag CHRISTIAN. His chestnut hair was unkempt, as he came to this meeting directly after a long day at work. He got up slowly, shaking his head in disappointment, and went outside toward his car, following the last of the crowd.

He heard cursing all around him and saw one of his fellow residents kick the side of the building in anger before one of the police officers locked the town hall doors. The internal motion-sensing lights turned off a moment later, leaving the building dark and empty.

Christian Reed stared at it briefly. "What happened to the town?" The town he had always called home. "When did everything become so complicated and corrupt?"

A cool breeze traveled through the parking lot, causing the flagpole atop Meadowsville Town Hall to make a distinct ringing sound. Christian looked up at the American flag, swearing that he saw someone standing next to it. He looked on momentarily but realized it was just the flag flopping around a bit but mostly remaining limp. The shadow that it cast must have been all that he'd seen.

Or was it?

Christian shook his head again, noting that the flag accurately represented the current political atmosphere in town. He convinced himself he was seeing things because he was tired from working all day and then attending the two-hour meeting. Christian got into his car to begin his short commute home.

* * *

As all the attendees of the meeting returned to their immaculate houses, the town quieted. The businesses, houses, and township buildings all went silent, almost in unison. Each and every building looked brand new in the moonlight, with spotless windows, fresh paint, and a picturesque appearance. Everything appeared so perfect on the outside of this place.

As Meadowsville settled for the night, a mysterious figure sat on top of the town hall, hiding behind the flag, peering down. It sported a long black coat, which further hid even the slightest glimpse of its appearance—Christian being the only one to notice it. A steady stream of mist ejected from the nose of the figure, contrasting the cool, early autumn weather, as it gently started to leap from rooftop to rooftop with ease, traveling throughout the town. Its town.

It admired the graffiti, reading MR. SMITH 4 EVER spray-painted on the sides of several buildings, with no attempts being made to clean it off. Several roaming gangs walked the streets with various weapons and attire. Each gang stayed to a particular area of town to protect their individual territories. They stayed away from each other to avoid conflict, but it still happened from time to time.

Cop cars patrolled all areas but purposely avoided the roads with activity. Their orders coming down from Chief Jones, taken directly from Mayor Wilkins, were to get involved only after an incident had happened or if something got too out of control. It was up to their judgment, which proved to be inadequately executed. None of them noticed the dark figure as it soared over them all, admiring the nighttime theatricality.

It moved over a suburban section of town, hearing hordes of young children saying their prayers:

God almighty, who lives above,
Hear my prayers and feel my love.
Please keep me safe until day's light,
Using every bit of your power and might.
As this town is plagued by a century old myth.
And that name we fear is Mr. Smith.

The figure watched each of the tiny remaining bedside lights turn off in the children's bedrooms before continuing its journey. It stopped on one house, showing particular attention to it as it watched over one of the residents, David Adams. After several minutes of pleasing silence, it continued on its way.

It landed on the ground at the base of Chrysanthemum Drive, which was a dirt road leading up a very tall hill into a large eerie patch of unoccupied woods. Due to the totally flat terrain of Meadowsville, this elevation could be seen from any point in town.

Several aged and broken-down police barricades were pushed to the sides of the road. A black van, with several teenagers screaming inside, sped past, not seeing the figure. The license plate was blocked out and the side of the vehicle had Tour of Terrors written poorly on it. This was one of the staple tourist activities that frequented the supposed home of Mr. Smith, which sat at the top of the hill. The branches and leaves danced all over, as if cheerfully greeting the figure approaching its dwelling.

It walked slowly up the hill to a large mansion. What used to be a prized piece of real estate was now nothing more than a dilapidated fossil. As the figure entered the house, tattered curtains blew in the wind and rotted furniture occupied the entrance, which lead into a large dining room. Several dark-finished chairs and an oversized dinner table remained in good condition in the middle of the room. A stairway, showing much wear but still stable, led to the upstairs.

The figure went upstairs, grabbing an aged violin hidden near a large picture window that led out onto a flat portion of the roof, overlooking over the town. The instrument had several deep scratches, and the walnut finish was almost completely worn off, yet the original strings remained intact. The bright full moon exposed the silhouette of a man. He smelled the night air, positioned himself to play, and began a flawless performance.

A pack of three mutated German shepherds pulled a dying buck into the front door, eating it as it moaned in the darkness. Each dog was unique, with different parts of their mouths and faces torn off, pieces of skin missing, and exposed muscle on their exaggerated frames. Their eyes were pitch black, and they showed no remorse as they fed.

They chomped the raw meat of the animal and devoured the deer's insides quickly and efficiently, covering themselves in the various bodily fluids of their prey. They groomed each other and left the remains, bones and a few splatters of blood that already began absorbing into the rotted floorboards. The trio traveled to the man's side, sitting obediently, listening to him play. The man finished his song as the dogs all howled in unison as they watch over the town.

Welcome to Meadowsville . . .

2

Christian

Later that night, Christian tossed and turned in bed, unable to get a good night's rest. He had a very lucid dream, remembering himself as a five-year-old child, when he witnessed his parents get taken from him by what he believed might have been Mr. Smith.

He lay in his dark bedroom, looking at the figures on his walls and ceiling projected from a small nightlight.

A loud crash coming from the kitchen startled him. He stood up, able to move only in slow motion, as was the norm in most of his dreams, and peeked out of his bedroom door. He saw his father drop to the kitchen floor as his mother stood there with a bloodstained shirt, her face resembling something he had seen in a monster movie. Her beautiful blue eyes were now blood-shot with enlarged pupils and were sunken into her swollen face. *While she still looked like his mother, she was not herself. Something was very wrong.*

A large, ominous figure overtook the light behind her. Two blazing red eyes peered over her shoulder and acknowledged Christian, who was now frozen in fear. Christian stood there trembling, unsure whether he could hold back the tears. The shadow slowly moved around his mother, beginning to advance toward him. The lights in the house turned off one by one as it neared, making it impossible to get a clear glimpse of what this thing looked like.

Christian ran back to his bed, pushing himself to be faster, but despite his efforts, he still moved like he was running through thigh-high mud. He was able to get to the bed, pulling the covers over his head. He lay shaking, praying, and hoping he would not be harmed. There was silence for a few seconds as he waited for the door to open, but instead the shadow was already in his room, looking down on him. It somehow entered the room so quietly that Christian didn't hear it.

The nightlight exposed nothing of the intruder as it hovered over the bed. Christian pulled the blankets up again, as if they were an impenetrable shield. As a large gnarled hand extended to pull the covers off, Christian heard his mother scream from the kitchen. The creature was gone before Christian could blink. The sound of his mother being killed was clear, and her screaming intensified, turning into crying, before her body joined his father's on the ground. The figure was gone, and the house was dead silent. But the cries continued somehow . . .

Christian jumped awake to hear his infant son, Adam, crying. Christian was panting and sweaty, trying to orient himself after the nightmare. He looked to his left side, where his wife, Rebecca, lay fast asleep. He attempted to wake her but recalled an earlier fight they had that day—

"You find every excuse not to be here with us," she said.

"It's not like that. I've lived here my whole life. I go to these meetings because I want to make things safe for us. For our family. I don't want Adam and Caroline to grow up like I did. This town needs us." He defended himself without taking any responsibility.

"We need you! Do you remember us?" she yelled.

"Maybe if your family wasn't worthless, they'd be around to help us out so you're not always holding my ass over the fire," he shouted back.

"And if yours—" but she quickly stopped herself, realizing she had taken things too far.

They both stayed quiet.

"Christian, I'm sorry. I didn't mean to go there."

"It's fine. Let's just be done with it," he said, walking away to go ready himself for bed, unable to reciprocate an apology to Rebecca.

Christian got up to take care of Adam, still feeling strong resentment toward Rebecca. They had these types of disagreements on a somewhat consistent basis, and he felt she both overreacted and was extremely accusatory toward him. Since his parents had been killed, Christian had been unable to fully trust anyone, his wife included. This, in his mind, made any type of apology obsolete, as he expected everyone to accommodate him in order to win his trust. This had plagued him both personally and professionally, and until he understood his portion of the issues, he would not be able to move on and improve himself. This was a long, difficult road for any individual, and Christian wasn't ready for it yet.

He passed his toddler daughter, Caroline, as she slept in her little bedroom. A tuft of curly red hair stuck out of several messy blankets and stuffed animals. He smiled at the sight of her and went to the next room to tend to Adam.

Adam lay on his back, wiggling and screaming, red in the face, and Christian empathetically cradled him. He reached down to fetch the chewed up green pacifier, putting it in Adam's mouth, but it had no marked effect on the infant's mood. Adam quickly spat it out onto the ground, and Christian was unable to bend over to get it again. Frustration and exhaustion set in, and Christian tried to control his breathing as the screaming overwhelmed him. He clenched his fist and tried to retain focus on his breathing, which was still not normalized after the nightmare. He rocked back and forth for what seemed like an eternity, eventually getting his one-year-old back to sleep. He put Adam down, looking adoringly at the vision of a peaceful night's rest. Adam's little face was a sight to behold. His little blue onesie, wide-open mouth, and bald head drooped to the left, with small trails of drool dripping down both cheeks, would make even the hardest of individuals express adoration.

"God, how I admire you, kid," Christian said, jealous of Adam's contentment.

Unable to return to bed, he paced quietly around the house, no longer afraid of the dark, which was something that took him many years to accomplish after his parents were murdered. He reached the living room and saw a picture of his parents and himself as a young boy. Even with all the years that had passed, not a day went by that he didn't miss them. He took the picture and sat on the armrest of the nearby couch. All three of them were smiling and jovial, enjoying the times when things were more simple and manageable. He yearned for that type of family dynamic once again for himself and also to protect his family so they did not have to endure the same injustice he suffered.

Unfortunately, the only family he and Rebecca had nearby were her parents, who had been dismissed from their household due to their constant abusive ways toward her and, to a slightly lesser extent, toward him too. Despite continually setting healthy boundaries, her parents worsened during the first few years of their relationship, and both Christian and Rebecca decided, as a combined effort, that their behavior was unacceptable and could no longer be tolerated. All communication was cut off. Only in an extremely dire situation, when all other options were exhausted, would they ever reach out to them for anything. Beyond that, it had been years since either party communicated with one another, and even after the birth of Adam, there was no outreach by Rebecca's parents.

Christian held a strong grudge against Meadowsville, as his parents' killer was never caught in the thirty years since the killings. He'd heard of other such situations that had gone unattended to by the town, most of which are unofficially blamed on the supposed Mr. Smith legend. Due to all of the constant peculiar things being perpetrated in the town, he was never able to fully decipher what was tangible versus fictional. Needless to say, despite the origin, Christian was deeply disturbed at how it was all considered commonplace in Meadowsville.

Christian found himself unable to move away. There was a strange pull that kept him there, somehow content in his current situation and mindset, as if the town were a part of him in some strong way. And until he changed the town, he would not be able to evolve either. He struggled to find the best method to achieve both ambitions, but knew that things would have to change at some point. If not, the future of Meadowsville would be uncertain, whether due to the alleged Mr. Smith or whatever legitimate real-world horror was actually occurring. Christian would not allow his town, or family, to be put in jeopardy.

3

David

"D avid," the teacher said, directing his attention toward the student.

The fifteen-year-old boy watched two squirrels chasing each other around a tree near the classroom, not hearing his teacher at all. He chuckled to himself, wishing he was outside doing anything other than listening to European history. He continued to enjoy his daydreaming.

"David, are you with us?" the teacher asked, causing some giggling in the class. "David," the teacher yelled, making him jump to attention.

"Yes sir. Sorry," David finally retorted.

"I know that this is boring for you, but stay awake or you'll be here with me every day this week after school."

"Understood, Mr. Harris."

"That was rhetorical," he responded.

"Okay," David commented back.

"Does it give you some satisfaction to always get the last word in?" the teacher taunted.

David waited a few seconds before the teacher turned back to the chalkboard and then said, "No." He hoped to get further get under his skin. Mr. Harris shook his head without looking back and continued with his lesson.

Coming down from the low-level confrontation and his daydreaming, David's chronic anxiety symptoms heightened to their normal levels. Even the slightest redirection by his teacher triggered these feelings in him. The paranoia set in, and he found it hard to keep himself in the present moment, as the room now felt distant. His thoughts began to race, his breathing pattern shifted to become shallower, and he felt jittery, wondering whether his classmates were laughing at him or just the situation. This was a problem David had dealt with most of his life, and he struggled to control the intense feelings.

Mr. Harris ended the class, reminding the students to stay seated for announcements.

"*Good morning, Meadowsville High! Today is looking like a great day. Sunny, cool, and we got lasagna being served at lunch! Yum, yum,*" the overcharged student exclaimed. "*The chess club has a meet after school today, and both the track and football teams must report to practice by three thirty sharp. No tardiness, you guys!*"

David was poked from behind by his best friend, Erik, who leaned over to speak to his comrade.

"Are you okay?" he asked. "You seem all pent-up today."

"Yeah, I'm fine. Mr. Harris is an asshole, and my dad was up before the ass crack of dawn, wrecking the garage just for fun. So I'm just tired today," David said, referring to his well-known family situation.

"That's rough. My pop is still sleeping off his hangover. We should bet on who can sleep the longest after each drinking bender." Erik joked about their equally unmannerly fathers, which was one of the many sources of their strong bond.

"And don't forget to be inside no later than nine sharp tonight. The town curfew is still in effect," the announcements continued. *"Have a great day, everyone!"*

"Erik, stop talking," Mr. Harris barked out.

Erik leaned back into his seat. "Can I go to the bathroom?" he asked.

Mr. Harris gave him a strong look of disapproval and tossed the taped-up hall pass to him. Erik looked at it and held it away from him like a piece of smelly garbage. He left the room and stood in the hallway flipping his middle finger in a myriad of ways toward Mr. Harris, who didn't see it because of the jackets hanging by the door. David tried not to laugh out loud, and the effort to do so helped control his anxiety quite efficiently, as his attention was no longer consumed by it.

An elderly female hall monitor confronted Erik and shut the door to the classroom so nothing could be heard. She asked him for his hall pass, pointing her wrinkled finger in his face. Erik purposely dropped it, asking her to get for him. As she bent over, he unzipped his pants and pretended to violate her from behind. The entire classroom saw the scene through the large window panel of the classroom door and began laughing.

The hall monitor stood up, not realizing what he was doing, and directed him to toward the bathroom, gently putting her hand on his shoulder. Erik motioned to his zipper being down, and she quickly removed her hand, knowing she couldn't touch him in that state. He walked away from her, leaving the woman with her hand on forehead, questioning why she still did this job with such obnoxious and disrespectful students.

Upon his return several minutes later, the bell rang to dismiss class. David laughed as he packed up his backpack and met Erik outside. Erik slid the hall pass across the entire room to Mr. Harris, who sat at his desk looking infuriated. Before David could say anything, Erik quickly got distracted by several girls wearing form-fitting clothing.

"Jesus Christ. It's not fair. Tonya's ass looks so perfect today. I'll catch you later," Erik said as he followed her down the hall.

"Class is this way," David called to him.

"Yep, I know," Erik responded, not turning around, continuing to follow the girl in the wrong direction. "I'll get there in a few. I'm just enjoying the view."

David smiled at his friend's impulsiveness. He turned and was bumped by an older student, who didn't apologize or acknowledge him.

"My mistake," David said sarcastically, noticing their MR. SMITH T-shirt. "Mr. Smith, what a crock of shit."

He walked to his next class and noticed other Mr. Smith paraphernalia in various forms around the school, ranging from attire to art projects and even spray-painted in the boy's locker room. It seemed to have increased lately, and David wondered why. While he wanted to believe in the myth, as it meant there was more to the world than he had a grasp on, he found it all highly questionable.

4

Game

A disheveled young woman stood in the dining room of her home. Blood dripped down her chin and fingertips as she shook. Barbara Wright's body felt like nothing she had ever experienced before. A satisfaction that could not be adequately described. She looked at her reflection in a window, seeing slightly enhanced facial features and large teeth sticking out of her mouth. Her blonde hair was in complete disarray, and her designer blouse was ruined with the crimson fluid coming off her full lips.

A soothing, guitar-dominant song played in the background, creating an ambience of intensity in the room.

You set my world ablaze
I'm awake and see nothing but you

She turned around, looking for someone, but she appeared to be alone. The music continued.

I refused to fall in love but then you changed it all
Such a nasty game to play

The woman looked at her wedding ring as the small diamond shone through the blood. She saw her husband, dead before her, with his wedding band also reflecting the same overhead light. Their marriage lasted only four months. They promised to give each other everything right out of college, and indeed this had proven that promise to be true, to an extreme never imagined.

She began to gag at the sight of what she had done to him and panicked. Her canines protruded out of her mouth even more. Her nails extended into claw-like protuberances, cutting through her nail beds. She screamed, losing the remainder of control over herself. She flailed and started destroying her house in a fit of rage.

"Why did you make me do this!" she screamed at an unknown perpetrator.

The woman saw a picture hanging up of her husband and her, which caused her to become unsure of her footing. She tripped and fell but was caught in the arms of a large man with a long black trench coat who suddenly emerged from the darkness of the living room. The same man who resided on Chrysanthemum Drive.

He held her, calming her briefly as they locked eyes.

Love makes you do such strange things
But as long as it's with you

The man lifted up his coat, enveloping the woman who was now fully engorged with the blood of her husband. He bit her neck, drinking every last bit of blood that came out. The music continued to play, and the man dropped the woman, vanishing as quickly as he appeared before the body even hit the floor. The couple lay next to one another, almost in the shape of a heart. Their smooth, youthful faces were angled toward each other as their hands somehow fell perfectly into one another, as if they were renewing their wedding vows in death.

Music continued to play as the night wore on.

5

Concern

That same night, David was home, working out in his basement gym. There was one light hanging from the ceiling and no windows, making it a very dark level of the house. The large basement had exposed pipes and wires in the high ceiling, with unpainted concrete walls and floor, making it resemble a dungeon. If not for the free weights and jump rope on the one end, it might have been mistaken for one.

The washing machine, dryer, and furnace were crammed into the opposite corner, also with a single light overhead, which David was forbidden to go near. His father's strict rules must be obeyed or David risked a number of punishments. While it was a convenience to utilize the space for his exercise regimen, his father let him do so just to give him some sense of control. He fully inspected the basement each time David was done, finding any reason to condemn him and make him feel like a privileged little brat.

David used to be afraid of this level of the house as a little boy. As he grew up, his mother would lock him down there to keep his father from finding him on certain days when he would drink too much. At a young age, David had to overcome his fear of the basement, which he not only accomplished but took over. David made it into his own space that he controlled and thrived in. Aside from the area of the basement with the furnace and such, the rest was his. Even though it was a secluded little area, it was his. And that was all that mattered. He now looked forward to going down there each day and taking out his aggressions on himself in total seclusion.

A light whistling was heard as David jumped rope at a fast pace. With no shoes on, he wore nothing but athletic shorts. His black undershirt was tossed in the corner of the room. Each time he made a mistake, the rope whipped his legs, bruising and cutting them. He didn't stop but rather ground his teeth and continued, despite the lashings initiating incredible levels of pain.

"Come on, keep it up," he told himself, tossing the rope aside as his toned body glistened from the single, tiny overhead light.

He wiped his hand through his saturated brown hair, sending sweat down his back. He picked up a large punching bag and tossed it across the room repeatedly, using different lifting techniques. Though he did his best to avoid the metal chain secured to the top that was meant to hang the bag, it occasionally whipped him on the bare back, cutting him.

"Avoid the chain or eat the pain," he said under his breath as sweat dripped into his mouth.

Once he became fatigued, he fell to the ground and began performing push-ups on his fists. He pushed himself off the ground with each repetition, punching the cement under him every time he descended. He reached total exhaustion and sat on the ground, a sweaty mess, trying to catch his breath. He thought back to his anxiety in school that day and used it all as fuel.

"Fucking bullshit," he said to himself, overcome by his anger.

Blood dripped down his fingers, a familiar sensation on his right hand. He quickly wiped it off the floor with his undershirt. If left untouched, it would create a terrible conflict with his father. A spotless basement was required at all times, and everything must be placed exactly the way he dictated too. Or else.

"I'm not good enough. I need to go harder," David said.

He tried to get up but fell back down. He was completely taxed.

"Why am I like this? Why can't I feel normal? Why can't Dad go away? Where are you?" he asked God, looking up toward the heavens.

He continued berating himself, allowing his mind to torture his body. He punched himself on the thigh several times in pure frustration, not realizing that a drop of blood accidentally landed on the beige-carpeted staircase.

Finally, able to get up, he drank some water and tossed his hands up, disappointed he didn't receive some kind of response from God. He tried hard each day to hold onto the dwindling bit of faith he had, but he found his motivation to believe in a higher power becoming increasingly hard, as his circumstances only seem to worsen.

He heard his father listening to him from behind the shut basement door. The labored breathing was much like a sick animal. David looked around frantically, now in a mild frenzy, ensuring everything in the gym was a certain way, to his father's liking, to avoid another conflict with him. David's anxiety symptoms were heightened once again.

He slowly went up the stairs and opened the door to see his father looming over the staircase. That big, intimidating figure just stood over him. After giving David an unsatisfactory glance, he ran past him, almost pushing David down the stairs. David regained his balance and prayed that he could get to his bedroom without incident. As he reached the doorway, his mother stood in the far corner of their immaculate kitchen, staring out of a window, looking very dismayed. A newspaper was left on the counter, showing an unflattering picture of Mayor Wilkins posing for one of her many election advertisements.

"Get your ass down here now!" David's father screamed.

David and his mother looked at one another.

"I didn't do anything, Mom. I swear," he pleaded with her.

"Then why is he calling me down there?" she replied, leaving David unsure who she was upset with.

"Mom . . ."

"David, this is an everyday thing with you two," she said, walking past him.

David tried to find the words to make things right, but he couldn't. His father continued yelling as his mother descended the stairs. David tried to control his anxiety and followed her. His mouth shook uncontrollably and his body tensed as the uneasiness overtook him. His father stood tall, sticking out his barrel-like chest, ready for a fight. His stained white T-shirt and ripped jeans somehow made him more intimidating.

"Come here now," he demanded as David walked to him timidly.

"Let me tell you one thing. In case you forgot. This is my fucking house. And these are my fucking rules. When I tell you to clean up this mess a certain way, you best listen," he exclaimed, shoving David backward, knocking him down. "Or you can get the fuck out. Simple as that. Go live on the streets like a piece of garbage."

David looked around one more time, trying to find what he missed, but came up with nothing. His father pointed to the drop of blood on the stairs.

"Clean it," he demanded, pointing at it.

David quickly took a rag to do so, but he was shoved backward by his father.

"Not you . . . her." He directed the task at David's mother.

She grabbed the cloth from David and began scrubbing, obviously exasperated.

"Now you. I see weights not facing forward. Fix it now, or you can forget about dinner again tonight. Do you want to starve?" he continued.

David walked past him, smelling a strong odor of alcohol No matter how many times that aroma invaded his olfactory sense, he was continually nauseated by it.

David and his mother finished their assigned tasks, under the supervision of their tormentor, and stood at attention, waiting for further instruction. This basement was no longer under David's control. His father has tarnished his achievement.

"Go to your room now," David was told.

He looked to his mother for some kind of support, but she continued looking down, keeping to herself.

David sprinted to his room, hearing his father tell his mother, "Ann, that kid of yours is a real piece of work. He's a fucking mistake. I didn't want kids, and you know that."

"That's enough. Stop it, Carl," she told him and walked away.

David locked his bedroom door behind him and grabbed a quick change of clothes. He waited about an hour for the sound of his parents' bedroom door slamming shut, signifying that his father had gone to bed.

David opened his window and crawled out onto the roof. A large shadow startled him outside, but when David stood up and looked again, there was nothing there. He started to question whether he was losing his mind, but the same mysterious figure who watched over him was indeed there with him. It just ducked out of David's sight. All the rumors over the years that he'd heard of John Smith and such were much like his faith in that he wasn't sure what to believe anymore.

David quickly ran to Erik's house several blocks away, ignoring the town curfew. Every home on his route was in superb order, with almost no imperfections to speak of. He reached the middle of Coral Rose Court and saw Erik on his front steps, looking distressed.

"Bad night for you too?" he asked his friend.

"You think?" Erik responded mockingly. "My dad deserves to get punched in the mouth some days. He thinks I drank some of his whiskey. He's just so hammered that he forgot it was him. Can you believe that crap?"

"Unfortunately, I can."

They briefly stood in silence.

"You wanna hit the courts?" David asked.

"Absolutely," Erik responded, perking up.

Erik grabbed a basketball from his front yard, and they walked, side by side, several blocks to the elementary school basketball court on Gladiolus Way. It was well past the nine o'clock curfew, and other than a few lights being on inside random houses, the town was quiet. Neither minded the potential dangers of a late night excursion in Meadowsville. The two had made a habit out of using nights like this to relax and get some of their frustrations out on the basketball courts. As they walked, they spot one of the well-established gangs of people, dressed up like superheroes, patrolling a few streets away from the school. The boys watched and made sure they weren't seen. The gangs didn't bother them unless they were doing something suspicious. It was rare that they fought amongst themselves too.

The boys forgot about their home lives and began play HORSE for a bit.

"You got H-O-R," Erik joked as David missed the first few attempts.

"Yep. Takes a HOR to know a whore," David clapped back.

They laughed and enjoyed each other's company, demonstrating just how strong their friendship was. Over all the years they'd known one another, despite any of the issues they faced, they could always depend on each other. Erik noticed that David had a more significant number of cuts and bruises all over his body than normal, as they continued to shoot hoops.

"What's going on there?" he asked with genuine concern.

David looked at his beaten-up legs, quickly dismissing the comment by responding, "Nothing. Just trying some new workout stuff."

"You gotta be more careful or someone is gonna notice all that."

"They already do. But they usually attribute it to me being athletic. Injuries happen, so it's fine."

David began to miss every shot, becoming noticeably rattled.

"You sure you're okay?" Erik asked.

"Yeah, I think so. Just another bad patch. I'll get through it," David said.

"Hang in. We only have a few more years and we can get outta here. We're almost halfway through tenth grade. So close to the end," Erik encouraged.

Sirens were heard nearby, and they stopped talking. Two squad cars rushed by the school with a trailing third turning into the courts, putting his spotlight on the boys.

"It's past curfew. Get home before I come back, or you'll both be in a shitload of trouble," the frantic officer yelled out his window, speeding off toward Barbara Wright's home. The lights briefly exposed David's watcher observing the boys from beyond the light of the courts, but neither noticed.

"Shit, short game tonight," Erik says.

"Guess so."

They walked slowly back home in silence. When they reached Lilac Lane, David's block, they pounded fists, and David went toward his house with the basketball.

"Hey, I know you like playing with my balls, but I do need them back at the end of the night," Erik joked.

David smiled, passed the ball to Erik, and they separated. David stood outside his house, looking through a window at his mother, who was sitting alone in the living room and reading. She stayed up late to avoid being in bed with David's father, and because she didn't work, she would sleep in late too.

David wished she would take him and move out but understood it would never happen. The two parents were completely immersed and codependent with each other, with David as a mere detail in their relationship. It hurt him to see his parents like this and how the three of them were glorified inconveniences to one another. David depended on Erik as a huge support, as he came from a very similar set of circumstances, but wished he could have someone to take him away from this misery and give him a new, more fulfilling life.

David climbed back onto the roof of his house but decided to sit there and enjoy the evening air. He again prayed to

God for help but expected and received no answer. Feeling the lingering discouragement, he went into his room. The sound of his father snoring echoed in the house and made it difficult for David to fall asleep. He woke up continually, although the soft playing of a violin soothed him to sleep from atop the house.

6

Memories

Almost a decade ago, Meadowsville remained largely the same.

A shadowy figure rested atop a tall tree branch, feasting on a raccoon. It looked over several quaint houses, one of which had a toddler playing outside in the backyard. As the animal was drained of all its blood, an unsatiated feeling remained. The creature disposed of the raccoon and descended toward the young boy like a spider coming down from its web.

It took note that the windows to the house were open and the boy's parents were in sight, so it was extra cautious to avoid being detected. The mother stood idly by as the father scarfed down his meal. He made a mess of the table, slammed his fists down, and yelled something to the mother. She nodded and began to clean up as the man poured himself a drink and stormed off.

"David, dinner in ten minutes," she yelled from inside.

"Okay, Momma," the boy responded as he sat, downtrodden, on the small swing set.

The creature landed just beyond the reach of the motion-sensing lights behind him, accidentally snapping a twig under his boot. He stopped in his tracks and waited to see whether the boy responded. David turned to look and lost his grip due to his father slamming a door from inside the house. He fell backward, scraping his arm on the chains of the swing set and bumping his head on the ground.

The figure positioned itself to grab the boy when David turned to look directly at it. All he could see were the eyes of the beast and the outline of a man. They both sat motionless as the figure whispered the name *Timothy* under its breath at the sight of the boy's face. He was clearly being reminded of something very sentimental. David rubbed his head and saw a slow-bleeding cut on his forearm. All thirst diminished for the figure, and he tried to speak but was unable to, still fascinated at the sight of the young boy.

David looked up with glossy eyes and asked, "Who are you?"

"My name is Blackheart," the man said with some hesitation.

"That's a funny name."

A large, toothy smile appeared on Blackheart's face.

"I like your jacket. Almost like a cape. I have one of those inside. I try to fly, but it doesn't work." David continued rubbing his head and looked at his arm again.

"I see you hurt yourself, David. Are you okay?"

"Yeah, I fell. Daddy slammed the door inside. He gets angry. He yells at me a lot."

"I know. He shouldn't though. You're a good boy."

David smiled.

"Can I show you how to make that feel better?"

David nodded.

Blackheart rolled up his left sleeve, exposing a scarred forearm, and lacerated it with one of his nails, making it bleed. He took a finger and ran it along the cut, collecting the majority of blood. He licked it and motioned for David to try.

David made an unsure expression but decided to try the approach. He first attempted, adorably, to lick the back of his forearm but failed and ultimately used his other hand instead. He wiped the blood and slowly tasted it.

He yelled, "Yuck." He rubbed his tongue on his shirt. "That's disgusting."

"Does it still hurt?" Blackheart asked, smiling again.

"Not much, no. Hey, you were right," David responded, smiling in delight.

"David, dinner is on the table. Let's go," David's mother yelled outside.

"I have to go, Mr. Blackheart. Thank you for helping me."

"Anytime, David. It was great meeting you."

David quickly ran inside the house and shoveled the small meal down his throat. He quickly ran to his room, locking the door behind him. There were no toys anywhere in the house except in his room. Blackheart noted that his bedroom was treated like a holding cell for David, while the rest of the house was put together to suit the needs of his father.

Blackheart left to feed more, but he could not take his mind off David. This boy awakened memories he had ignored for decades. Memories of Timothy.

As the night progressed, Blackheart later returned to check on David, who was struggling to sleep. Blackheart brought with him a beautiful violin. The instrument was neatly polished, displaying worn ebony fingerboards and pegs. Blackheart played it so softly, only he and David could hear the music. This instrument was taught to him under inhumane circumstances but had, over time, transitioned into a personal grounding practice. He was thrilled to see that it had a similar calming effect on David, who quickly fell asleep to the rich, warm sounds.

At times, over the following months, David yelled out "Thank you" to his guardian. As the years progressed, David didn't even realize the violin sounds were still there, and he forgot about his meeting with Blackheart. Blackheart continued to watch over him almost every night from that point forward, showing signs of having a deep yearning for David's companionship one day.

When the time was right.

7

Faith

That weekend, David lit the candles on the altar during the church service as the congregation looked on. He struggled as the wicks were burned down too low, but he managed to get them all lit. He looked out the stained glass windows and saw the small houses nearby with the driveways full of cars. They all got to sit at home while he was stuck in the Church of Christ against his will. It was a place that sat on the western portion of Meadowsville on a tiny property that housed the church, a large parsonage, and a playground consisting of a slide and a single swing. This place made David doubt his faith more than anything else.

Pastor Murphy approached him from behind and aggressively whispered with a slight lisp, "We went over this how many times? Light them from right to left. Do it properly, boy."

David brushed him off, refocused, and lit the final candles on the altar. He attempted to walk off the side of the altar to his chair but was physically redirected to the front opening. Pastor Murphy rolled his eyes as several members of the church giggled at David's expense.

David took his seat, and the pastor stared down at him with a very smug look on his face before starting the service. David sat with his head slightly lowered, praying independently, hoping the service ended quickly so he could leave.

God, please hear me. I've prayed to you countless times now. Please give me any sign that you're there and haven't forgotten about me. He prayed to himself, hoping for an immediate response.

Again, he received no obvious divine intervention and grimaced to himself. He looked up to see his mother in the back row, gabbing with some of her friends, cheerful and giddy. She forced him to attend church, despite illness or religious objections, so she could have an excuse to leave the house and avoid his father, who refused to attend himself. While David appreciated the attention, he did not enjoy being used as a ploy.

* * *

Also in the congregation was Christian's family. Rebecca and Caroline sat in the row ahead of David's mother while Christian stood in the back corner wearing Adam in a harness, rocking him to sleep.

Caroline turned around and showed her father a picture of several circular smiley faces and told him it was a family portrait. He smiled and tried to pay attention to the hollow sermon but had trouble focusing on it. Adam napped with his head backward, drooling all over the harness. Christian cherished moments like this with his family.

Caroline jumped out of her seat and ran down the side aisle, laughing. Rebecca tried to catch her but wasn't fast enough. She almost ran up to David, who was in deep thought. She startled him, and they locked eyes with each other. Caroline stopped quickly, looking at him fearfully, allowing her mother to grab her. She carried Caroline back to their seats, softly apologizing to everyone for the disruption as her husband tried to hide his laugh. Rebecca sat and looked at Christian as they both chuckled, totally embarrassed.

* * *

The service later concluded, and David returned home with his mother. The entire thirty-minute ride home was in complete silence. Their relationship had been strained by the stressful situation at home, and while they were normally civil with one another, there were certain times when they chose to be silent as opposed to bickering. As David got older and became more inquisitive with his mother, she began closing herself off to him in order to keep from being condemned by her only son. She felt a high level of guilt for not having the confidence in herself to leave his father. As David made more logical points as to why she could leave for both of their sakes, she struggled more and more to defend how staying was a better alternative. She loved Carl and held out hope that he would change one day. She was conflicted in knowing that whatever she did, she would hurt either David or her husband, so she chose to remain in her current predicament.

They arrived home, and the front door was wide open. They cautiously got out of the car and entered, seeing the entire downstairs in disarray. Furniture was flipped over, broken dishes were in the kitchen, and an empty bottle of vodka sat on the dinner table. David's father was sequestered in his bedroom, passed out, clearly having had another outburst.

"Mom, I can't do this anymore," David said, incensed.

"David, I know. I know," she responded passively.

"No, I don't think you do," he argued.

"You know how he grew up. He drinks and does these things because he can't help it. He used to get beaten every day by your grandfather."

"That's no excuse. He should get help."

"He doesn't believe in it."

"So we have to suffer like this?"

"I don't know what to tell you. No one is leaving, and that's that. And he can keep threatening you with getting kicked out, but it's not going to happen. Just deal with it and don't let it bother you. Now, are you going to help me clean up, or am I doing this myself?"

"I just don't get this, Mom. I never have and never will," David replied, the little optimism for his mother now gone.

He walked over and gave her a hug as they began moving the furniture back in place and picking up the broken items on the floor. Despite their disagreements on the living situation, they still loved each other.

David helped her finish and retired to his room later that evening. He sat on the floor and felt a still healing wound on his right palm from his last workout. He began to tug at it until it opened back up and bled. The pain gave him incentive to pull harder, as he grit his teeth, enjoying the discomfort. He then took a hunting knife and cut his left palm, repeating the activity on the other hand. He sat, feeling the blood pool in both palms, and began to pray again.

"God, I'm done asking you for help. Have it your way and enjoy the show."

He pulled off his shirt and started wiping the blood across his body in a ritualistic manner. He was tired of feeling out of control. He would now take charge of his own destiny whether God agreed with his actions or not.

Blackheart watched from the roof next door with great concern.

8

Conflict

Across town that same night, Christian stood in his backyard splitting large pieces of wood. He admired his new ax and struck each piece in anger. Beads of sweat bounced off of him with each hit, and he didn't flinch even as the splintering wood chips hit him.

Upper management had just informed him that one of his employees resigned and he would be responsible for filling the later shift, in addition to his regular day shift at the Meadowsville Market. His wife would now have to be responsible for her full-time work schedule and also picking up and dropping off both children at daycare.

He dropped the ax and began tossing the prepared wood into the pile next to his house. The emerging sound of marching got closer, and he looked up to see his local neighborhood watch group approaching. All eight men were holding small arms and dressed in military fatigues. They were a friendly group, consisting of fellow fathers and, in two cases, grandfathers, Christian had known for years.

"Evening, fellas," he said, catching his breath.

"Christian, how the hell are ya?" the portly leader of the group yelled out.

"Well, Bob, I'm hanging in. The struggle is real, brother," he said, smirking.

"We don't mean to be a bother, but you really shouldn't be out here like this alone. It's well past curfew, and who knows what might be lurking around. If not those goddamned hellhounds, could be those stupid kids dressed up like God knows what, just looking for a problem or whatever else," Bob said.

"Yeah, I know what's out here at night. You guys, apparently," Christian responded, and a few of the men laughed at the comment.

"You're not afraid of what's out there? You're really not afraid of Mr. Smith?"

"No, I'm not. There's plenty of real things to be afraid of in this world. I don't have much time for fictional things," Christian replied with a brief pause, not fully convinced of his reply. "I'll be fine though, guys. Really. Never had a problem in all these years. I appreciate the concern and what you all do for the neighborhood."

"You still sure we can't convince you to join up?" Bob said, referencing several prior attempts to recruit Christian.

"No, I'm okay. But if you guys need anything, please be sure to let me know."

"Not a problem, but remember the offer is always there if you change your mind."

A loud howl from one of town terror's dogs interrupted the pleasantries. Despite not knowing his true name—whether it was Mr. Smith or someone else—the men knew the calling cards of this mysterious creature's presence.

"Welp, looks like we should get back to patrolling, Christian. You and the family have a good night. Be safe."

"Thanks, guys. Be careful and give 'em hell out there." The two men shook hands, and Christian gave a respectful nod to the remainder of the group.

Christian watched the men continue on and struggled with himself, wondering whether to join a good cause like that or wait for another opportunity. While he wanted to help the town, his resentment for it was still strong, and that jaded his personal process on the matter. Becoming unsure of his mindset, he went inside and tried to dismiss his frustrations.

He went to his bedroom and saw Rebecca reading with her glasses on. She was cuddled up with several blankets, but her shapely and appealing form was hidden beneath cheaply made pajamas.

"The kids asleep?" he asked.

"Yeah, they're down for the night," she responded, not looking up.

"Thanks for taking care of that, honey."

"I didn't mean to snap at you earlier. I know that you can't control what the marching orders are at the store. It's just going to make it really hard for me with this new schedule," she said, sliding her glasses down and putting her book aside.

"Appreciate it," he replied, not fully accepting her words.

"We'll make it work. We always do," she assured him, going back to her reading.

Christian smiled at her as he took off his shirt, exposing a soft yet muscular upper body. He leaned over and kissed her forehead, hoping to pique her interest in sex.

"Is this doing it for ya?" he asked playfully.

"As good as you look, I'm not touching you until you shower," she responded.

"Too dirty?"

"Too dirty," she replied. "But good try, Daddy." She returned to her book again.

"So after I shower then?"

"Maybe not tonight. Can I take a rain check or do you really need it?"

The wind was taken out of his sails, but Christian light-heartedly mocked the infrequency of their intimacy as he went into the shower. "Oh well, I tried. See you again in a few weeks."

They smiled at the friendly banter as they went about their individual business. Both remembered the days when their intimacy was much more frequent and passionate. The current obligatory romps were just maintenance for the relationship. While satisfying, they were functional and nothing else. The lack of support around them put a tremendous load on both Christian and Rebecca. Their focus and energy levels were obliterated by the end of each day. They both wondered whether things would continue like this or not.

9

Ignorance

The town reservoir was being cleaned up by a group of three public works department employees. One was an older gentleman, Joe, looking at retirement within the next few years, along with his middle-aged subordinate, James, and a brand new young worker, Johnny. It was a muggy day, and the smell from the reservoir was revolting.

"So what the hell is all this?" Johnny asked, observing the buildup of debris in the water.

Joe jumped in and started pulling out deer bodies and other random animal carcasses from the water, tossing them onto the dirt road the other two men stood on. James and Johnny, wearing torn work gloves, begin taking the parts and loading them into the back of their spotless DPW-branded pickup truck for proper disposal.

"This is fucking disgusting. What the hell dumps dead animals in here?" Johnny asked.

"Would you shut up and keep working," Joe called out.

"No, don't tell the boy that. Work slower. Collect that overtime. My Lexus needs new tires," James said, moving very slowly on purpose.

Johnny started gagging at the putrid smell coming from the bodies.

"Ten dollars that he pukes within the hour," Joe yelled to James, who started laughing.

"No, really. What does this?" Johnny asked.

"Mr. Smith," James said.

"Nope, it's those fucking wolf hybrid things out there. You've heard the howling. Luckily, they keep to the woods," Joe said, spitting to the side, getting nauseous from the odor of the scene.

"So why does anyone stay here? There's other places to live that're safer," Johnny suggested.

"High wages, low living expenses, and everyone you work with is dumb as dirt, so you always feel great about yourself. Especially with old dogs like Joe," James joked.

Joe heaved a half-eaten coyote at both men, and the water splattered onto their faces. Both quickly wiped it off.

"The other positive thing about living in Meadowsville . . . all these animals getting killed. You won't ever clip a deer in your car or anything," James said.

"Yeah, but what if those things attack someone?" Johnny asked.

"You'll hear a lot of crap out there about cover-ups and missing persons and all that. Most of it is hearsay. We have so many people in and out of town, there's always going to be some rumors. But you check any of the records—this town is one of the safest out there. And it's the size of a small city. Like seventy or eighty thousand people, I think, nowadays. That's pretty impressive when you think about it," James said.

A supervisor pulled up to the group with his window down and a big, burly arm hanging down to the side. His hand was darker than dirt, as he rarely washed it on the job.

"Hey, ladies. Do me a favor and get back to work. I sign the overtime slips based on what you actually deserve, not what you think you deserve. Now load those animal parts up and go scatter them by the graveyard for the tourists to see. You know the deal," he called out to the three workers.

The group quieted down and continued to load the animal parts, clearing out the blockage after several hours. The department of public works employees, like the police, was under certain orders to place animal parts found at specific locations, leave graffiti that pertained to Mr. Smith, and other such aesthetics to keep the legend strong and the money from tourism pouring in. With the extremely generous compensation all of the town employees received for their efforts, they displaced any uncertainty about what they were told to do. There was an overly detailed codicil in all of their contracts that they were all subject to very harsh penalties if they spoke out about certain more specialized job details like this.

10

Transition

David stood in front of his English class, shaking uncontrollably and becoming increasingly disoriented as he tried to finish reading his book report. Each time he opened his mouth, it shook, and the tightness in his locked abdomen didn't permit him to breathe or pronounce anything coherently. Several beads of sweat trickled down his face as he questioned whether he was going to pass out or not.

"David, are you going to talk or just stand there dancing all day?" Mrs. Larson teased.

The entire class erupted in laughter, sending David into complete panic.

"Go collect yourself and come back to finish," the teacher told him.

David rushed out of the room.

"Anyone else want to volunteer? We have nowhere else to go but up after that," Larson kidded as David was still within earshot.

David heard the dismissal bell and rushed out of the school a few minutes later.

"That was it. This is for you," he said aloud to God, with a plan clearly in mind.

He walked past Billy D's Bar and Grill in the middle of town, and saw Mr. Smith drinks free here on Tuesdays, and so do the ladies, plastered across the windows.

He thought about how foolish the township lore was and anyone who believed in Mr. Smith. He never once understood the fascination with such a ridiculous idea.

Erik ran up to David and grabbed him by the shoulder. "Hold up, kid. Why didn't you wait for me? What's wrong," he asked.

"I don't wanna talk about it. I just wanna go home," David told him, fighting back tears.

Erik became uneasy as he saw the distress in his friend's eyes.

"Hey, um . . . come over to my place for a bit. My parents aren't home for a few hours. It'll be fun. You don't have anything else to do," Erik asked.

"No, really. I'm okay."

"Come on. We haven't gamed in a few weeks."

David slowed down and agreed to go, despite not wanting to. He just didn't want to alarm Erik as to his intentions for later that evening.

They walked to Erik's house, allowing David to resolve the remainder of his panic attack symptoms. He and Erik played various video games for hours, not speaking much, as Erik kept stalling David from leaving, out of pure concern for his best friend. Once the sun set, David came to peace with what his plans were for that evening.

"I'm getting tired. I need some rest." He fibbed to Erik.

Erik noticed the deep, fresh lacerations on David's palms and grew more disturbed.

"You sure you're okay?" Erik asked one last time, not able to look away from the wounds.

"I will be. Thanks for everything," David said, grabbing his backpack and leaving in a hurry.

David left, and Erik stood at the window, watching him hastily walk off.

"Something's not right here. I gotta go get him," he said to himself, putting on his sneakers.

As Erik left, his parents pulled up and reprimanded him for leaving so close to the town curfew. He tried to keep an eye on David, who was now too far away to be seen, and his parents momentarily prevented him from getting past them.

David walked slowly, smelling the brisk nighttime air and contemplating various ways to commit suicide. He began to tear up, still waiting for God to save him, but nothing happened. He had lost the remaining bit of faith in Him, and between his situation at home, his worsening anxiety, being teased at school and church, and all of the stressors he had, he had reached his threshold. It did not get better, and he was tired of fighting. It'd been too long and too many things had happened, and suicide was the only way he felt he could end all the suffering in one act. He wanted to find peace for himself, even if it meant dying. This was truly going to be the end, and it would be by his own choice. He no longer respected God enough to make the decision for him anymore.

David heard something flapping in the wind behind him. He turned to see the shadowy figure with his signature trench coat moving fluidly in the wind. David saw his face but didn't remember who he was after their initial meeting when he was a child.

"Who are . . ." David said but stopped himself before finishing the sentence. A slight feeling of recognition swept over him, but he couldn't figure out why.

The two stared at each other for a minute before David turned and ran, trying to reach his home. Despite how hard he pushed himself and how fast he sprinted, the sounds were consistently right behind. Like David wasn't moving at all. This creature was going to do what it wanted to David, and he had no choice but to accept it. He finally stopped and turned, feeling more scared than ever before. The man from his childhood stared down at him with a paralyzing intensity.

"It's you. It's really you. You do exist," David whimpered, now fully believing in the Mr. Smith lore.

Smith—or whoever—grabbed David and punctured his neck with two large canines, drinking his blood. David tried to yell, but a heavy weakness overtook him. The droplets of his attacker's blood, originating from his now severed gumline, which had expanded for the exaggerated teeth to grow in, flowed into David's bloodstream. His body responded quickly to the fluid and began to change. The special substance in the blood created something ugly and abnormal. Something preternatural.

Erik came up on the scene, accidentally running into both of them, knocking David out of his captor's grasp. As the man's teeth were taken out of David's neck, they tore at his skin, making his blood pour out like a fountain. As Erik stood up, he saw David lying on the pavement, bleeding all over himself. The furtive man vanished.

"Oh Christ. Oh my God," Erik said, trying to use his jacket to stop the bleeding.

Erik was yelling for help when David became aware of his surroundings again. He became completely grounded over the next minute, but his body reacted to something Erik now exuded. There was a scent that was overwhelming, and David could almost hear the blood rushing through Erik's rapidly beating heart. This hunger needed to be satiated, and Erik was what it needed to quench the undeniable thirst. David tried to control himself, but his body moved, and he almost snapped Erik's forearm into two pieces with a single bite. Erik yelled, but David remained latched on, holding him in place. He drank Erik's blood and felt more strength with each drop of it, not caring about the ensuing struggle. He managed to stop himself and tried to spit the blood out as he became fully aware of what just happened.

"David . . . wait . . ." Erik whimpered as David ran off.

David sprinted with incredible speed, all of his senses heightened like never before. He ran through the elementary school and into the woods behind it. As he ran, feeling more upset than anything, he tripped over a large downed tree and landed face-first into some leaves. He looked up slowly and saw three hideous German shepherds standing before him. Each dog was equally terrifying, despite their varying distorted features. One had half of its face torn off, exposing its soft tissue. The other had several large patches of skin missing around its eyes and midsection. The last had no sign of skin or hair on its head or the left side of its body.

David noticed a dead deer in front of them, fully intact. One dog nudged it toward him, and they all walked away as if being ordered to do so. David smelled the animal and found it similar to Erik but slightly less appetizing. He began to bite at different parts of it, taking in the blood like a starved animal, trying to cope with what was happening. He was different now, and his body now needed blood however it could get it.

"David . . . what is this?" Erik, who held his mangled arm, slowly approached and fell to his knees beside David.

Erik experienced a similar transformation to David. The pain started to diminish and his energy refocused on the imminent feeding off the animal. His body had an immediate sense of vigor when his arm stopped bleeding and healed itself quickly. Erik began to feast on the deer with his friend, and they developed an astounding new bond. As they ingested more blood, their bodies began to repair and fill with energy.

Blackheart watched them from above, standing on a solid tree branch, blending into the night.

11

Brotherhood

One night several weeks earlier, Erik and David played video games in Erik's bedroom, enjoying each other's company as they had for more than a decade. While not brothers by blood, they were closer to each other than anyone else in their lives.

"I wonder why your dad likes me so much?" Erik asked.

"He's clearly got bad taste," David replied.

"You got a smart mouth on ya. You know what we do to smart mouths in the pen?"

David pinned Erik in the wrestling game.

"Let me guess. You lie down like a bitch. Just . . . like . . . that." David threw the words in Erik's face.

"You got lucky. Oh wait. You've never been laid. I take that back."

David got quiet.

"Dude, you scared of it? Like it's gonna bite you or something? Just feed that kitty your mediocre little salami and finally become a man," Erik continued, trying to lighten the mood.

David shook his head but didn't respond.

"We call it a red snapper. But you see, that's just an expression. It doesn't actually snap. You dig?"

"You know the story there. I'm not like you with that stuff," David said, breaking his silence.

"Well, you can't always be a first round pick like me. But you'll learn. Eventually. Hopefully."

"Sure, sure," David said.

"Well, what about Stephanie?"

"What about her?"

"You think she cares about the rules of volleyball? She was tossin' it in your face hard the other day in gym class like I've never seen before."

"Oh, stop." David tried to bypass his friend's remarks again.

"She'd pretty much have to sit on your face to make it any more obvious."

"Yeah, maybe you're right. I guess. I dunno. It's hard to not be anxious around girls. My head gets too busy, and my body is just uncomfortable."

"Or you can just keep avoiding girls and prove your dad right. He bet me fifty dollars you're gay last week."

"We can't all be a walking STD like you. I'd love someone to swab your undies and put it under a microscope. They're bound to find all sorts of new bacteria. Probably start a new civilization from your ball sweat."

Erik laughed out loud.

"Is it really worth the effort though? Like is sex that good?"

"Well, lemme explain . . . yes. Yes, it is," Erik said with a serious face, which made David smile.

Erik won the next match as the two continued their trash-talking to one another.

"Sex is pretty amazing. But all kidding aside, it's just a part of shit. You should be into the girl too. Like, once you have sex, you've sort of peaked with that person. Not the kind of thing you want to ruin by rushing into. The connection is most important." Erik offered sincere advice to his inexperienced friend.

"Why do you do it so much?"

"The same reason that they keep sticking me in those retard classes. I'm a slow learner."

"I can always depend on you to help me when I'm down. And by help, I mean kick me."

They continued playing and having fun late into the night.

12

Loss

avid and Erik looked at each other as the deer was left in a heap. Both were mangled and unsure of what exactly had happened. They needed further nourishment. There was something else that was now present in their bodies. A foreign substance now fully integrated in their bloodstreams.

"What happened to us?" David asked, admiring his enlarged hands and dagger-like nails.

"Who was that?" Erik asked, referring to David's attacker.

Neither boy responded. David and Erik observed each other as if seeing for the first time. Their facial features were unrecognizable, their bodies exaggerated, and they could hear each other's hearts racing. All sounds, sights, and senses were now in overdrive, overwhelming both. David did his best to practice his breathing and was better able to do so.

Erik, on the other hand, had no experience managing anxiety-like symptoms and was less nourished, so he became unable to control himself. His eyes darted back and forth as he was overstimulated. David took note and tried to talk him down but was unsuccessful.

"This feels good. Real good," Erik said with a now deeper voice.

He stood up and pushed over a large rock nearby with ease. Feeling accomplished from the feat of strength, he yelled into the night in a tribal manner.

David flinched and was unsure of what to do.

"Erik, let's chill out for a minute. We can figure this out. Just give me a minute to sort this out."

"No," Erik quickly cut him off. "We've spent our entire lives dealing with scumbag parents, all that bullshit at school, and everything else. We've earned some time to enjoy ourselves. Let's have some fun. We can think later," he spouted, leaping out of the woods toward the neighboring baseball field. David pleaded for him to wait and ended up following him. They sprinted across the field, jumping over fences, Erik turning it into a foot race, with David just trying to restrain his friend so things did not spiral out of control. David caught up and tackled Erik as they rolled with tremendous momentum, crashing through the fence separating the field and playground.

"Come on, please stop for a minute," David said, trying to hold Erik down.

Erik snarled a bit, pushing him off.

"Cut it out," Erik said, physically becoming a bit more intimidating.

They stared at each other like animals competing for territory. Both braced themselves for the other to attack, but neither did anything. The standoff was interrupted when they heard laughter and chatter across the school grounds with their amplified hearing. A small group of older high school students ran around with flashlights. Some wore masks, while others had their faces painted, but all wore very expensive, name-brand sneakers. Another prime example of the privileged lives the Meadowsville residents had due to the prosperous local economy. All of the students were carrying baseball bats, clearly being one of the roaming gangs that strolled around the streets of Meadowsville each night.

"Mr. Smith? Where are you?" one of them, wearing a Meadowsville Maulers jacket, yelled out in a sarcastic tone.

"If we can get one good picture of him, the paper pays out," one of them said as the group briefly separated from each other to wander.

"Some guy from all the way in Oklahoma won two thousand dollars last year. And someone from Vermont fifteen hundred before that," another student exclaimed.

Erik smiled at David and asked whether he wanted to toy with them. Before David could say anything, Erik shoved him backward, knocking him down, creating a solid indentation of David's body in the moist grass. David jumped up quickly enough to see Erik take a huge leap and land on the roof of the one classroom, right above the one lone student. Erik dangled himself off the roof with one arm, waiting for the student to stumble into him. The student turned and came within a few inches of Erik, who roared in his face with an unmatched intensity, exposing his gargoyle-like features. The student screamed and instinctively stabbed Erik in the shoulder with a small knife he had latched to his pocket. Erik sniffled at the pain and dropped down, feeling the blood on his shirt. As he lost blood and used his powers carelessly, he continued to feel more like an animal and less like himself. David stood frozen, hoping Erik stopped himself, but realized he had to intervene before anyone got hurt.

Erik's voice changed to a very serious tone. He roared again and punched the boy into the brick wall behind him, almost knocking him unconscious as the rest of the students ran up to the chaotic scene. Erik lunged at them, but David arrived to hold him back. The students all dropped their weapons, grabbed their fallen friend, and quickly escaped, slipping and falling as they rushed off.

"What are you doing? He stabbed me," Erik yelled, trying to pursue them.

"You gotta stop. This isn't right," David said, using all of his strength to hold Erik back.

"Who the fuck made you the boss?" Erik said, pushing David off.

Erik knocked aggressively into David with his shoulder, but neither budged from the impact. They stared each other down again, for the first time seeing each other as polar opposites.

With their brotherhood now split, Erik snapped his teeth to taunt David, looking to fight.

"We don't have to do this," David pleaded, clenching his fist. "Don't do this."

Erik attempted to punch David, who grabbed him by the arm, swinging him through one of the large nearby classroom windows. The glass shattered, and David struggled to not enjoy hurting his friend. He yelled, feeling himself start to transform more as his frustration increased.

"Erik, slow it down. I didn't mean to hurt you." David's voice quivered as his body overwhelmed his mind.

Erik stood up as his previously bitten arm continued to bleed.

"It's okay. I know you just want to—" Erik threw a large handful of glass shards at David's face, cutting him. "Overthink things like you always do."

David wiped the glass off of him, his body growing into a larger form, and he asked Erik one final time, "Please, don't make me do this."

"Well, we never settled our score. We each had a victory over the other in the game. Let's have a real match now," Erik challenged, grabbing David's shirt and throwing him onto the playground, sending mulch up in the air like a bomb exploding.

David rolled several more times, landing hard against a large elm tree.

"Okay, you want it. You got it," David growled out.

Both transformed fully into their own unique-looking monsters and embraced their new selves. Their bloodshot eyes and pitch-black pupils matched one another as their bodies responded to the growing conflict. Their mouths were fully enlarged, and each tooth was now sharpened and elongated, especially the canines near the front.

They charged one another. David slashed Erik across the face. Erik became even more unstable and kept shaking his head, unable to harness his powers. They traded blows several times, with Erik's face having portions of skin taken out by David. Erik dropped to one knee, punching David square in the mouth, splitting his lip and causing a stream of blood to fly up across his forehead. David touched the wound but didn't acknowledge much pain. He then realized the more he used his powers, the less control he had and the more his thirst for blood increased. It was too late for logic now. He needed to fight for his life. Each of them knew only one person would walk away from this.

They tackled each other, rolling across the mulch and into a metal swing set. David struggled to get up, but Erik stomped the back of his head, sending his face directly into the dirt. David lay there, not able to see straight. Erik grabbed the chains from a swing and wrapped them around David's neck, stepping on his back and pulling in an attempt to strangle him. Short of air, David was able to kick backward, hyperextending Erik's right knee and knocking him down.

Erik screamed out in pain and tried to stand to reposition his knee but kept going back to the ground. His leg was completely fractured to the point of not being able to repair itself. Blood trickled down all but one of Erik's limbs at this point.

David kicked him in the abdomen, and Erik smashed into the still standing frame of the swing set as it collapsed on him. The metal poles connected with each other, sending out loud rings for people to hear blocks away.

David walked over, took one of the loosened metal pieces, and began beating Erik with it, not feeling any bit of guilt or regret. His logic and senses were fully subdued at this point. He needed to hurt his friend, which was something he never imagined. This foreign blood in his body had changed him. He was no longer anyone's victim, which was how he had felt for his entire life. He was now a predator.

Erik knocked the bar out of David's hands and was finally able to stand up on his own power. This was a brief accomplishment. He stumbled into David, his leg still completely debilitated, and tried to punch him again. He attempted to bite David's neck as they both tumbled down and the final struggle ensued. Some of the blood coming out of Erik's arms dripped into David's mouth, giving him the ability to deliver one more plea to his brother. They would be lost in this world without each other.

David, now sounding more animalistic than human, cried out, "Please . . . stop." A single tear fell down his battle-damaged face as some of his humanity was expressed. He realized how far the fight had gone and knew that it couldn't be stopped.

David gave up, struggling with the balance between his newfound powers and emotions, allowing Erik to overpower him. He didn't care if he lived or died and wouldn't be able to live with himself if he killed anything, including and most important, Erik.

Erik sank his teeth deep into David's neck. David closed his eyes, unsure of what to expect, and waited to die. He was surprised when Erik released his bite. David opened his eyes and saw nothing in front of him. Erik was gone, and the only sound was a jacket floating in the slight breeze behind him. David rolled over slowly and saw Blackheart holding Erik like an infant, who struggled to get free. Blackheart's strength was displayed as he held Erik with a single hand, unfazed by the movement. With great ease, he grabbed both of Erik's shoulders and pulled him vertically in half, creating a rainstorm of blood as the two halves plopped onto the ground. David cried out as Blackheart disappeared into the night.

David crawled to his friend and was forced to lick the bloody mulch to avoid losing consciousness from being so depleted. He did not know how to control his powers but did know that blood was what the body needed to feel better. As he regained more control, his cries became more human as he mourned over his fallen friend. He looked down at the lifeless halved face of Erik and buried his head in his hands, sobbing uncontrollably. He was now truly alone.

David didn't realize how loud his cries were. He accidentally alerted several nearby gangs of his whereabouts. He heard them arrive in the school parking lot, just on the other side of the playground. The first group arrived, all wearing various monster masks, armed with swords, hockey sticks, and golf clubs. A second group came from the opposite direction, wearing acolyte robes, armed with sharpened, weaponized wooden crosses. David crawled behind a large tire structure in the playground, smothering his cries, watching the scene unfold.

"This is our territory! You holy rollers aren't allowed on this end of town," the one representative yelled from the masked bunch.

"God has no boundaries. Either you are a believer of our cause or you are no better than John Smith," a member of the opposite side rebuked.

They two groups started battling as if their common purpose to protect the town was a nonfactor. They just needed an excuse to hurt one another, using Mr. Smith as a scapegoat to justify their misdeeds. They fought for several minutes, with members of each side being injured, before a police car drove by the school. The officer slowed, looking at the gangs, and continued on without interfering, waiting until the battle was complete before getting involved. The masked gang defeated their opponents and celebrated wildly as the last remaining ambulatory members of the other side retreated.

David continued to observe quietly, looking back and forth between the battle and Erik's remains, and lost consciousness several minutes later.

13

Discovery

Christian walked through the Meadowsville Market. He was the last person left in the building. A large clock in the middle of the store struck nine o'clock, signaling the beginning of the nightly curfew.

"Thank God," he said after completing another fifteen-hour day. "At least the paychecks are worth this crap."

He began shutting down the store, setting the alarms, and turning off the lights.

"Yeah, this is so much better than spending time with my family," he mumbled.

He read the large banner over the deli's precooked foods section, JOHN SMITH'S FAVORITE PRIME RIB NOW JUST $15.99, and sighed at the disgusting amount of publicity for the town's favorite legend.

He grabbed a leftover bag of garbage behind the deli and took it to the back alley on his way out. He locked the door and tossed the bag into the large dumpster. A loud thud let him know it landed, but he heard an odd noise from the other side of the receptacle. He picked up a loose piece of wood for protection and slowly peered around to see what was there.

Christian saw a fully transformed David, heavily injured and in noticeable pain. He heard some mild grunts and observed the massive sharp teeth penetrating an expired, maggot-ridden package of meat. Christian took a deep breath, unsure of what he was seeing in that moment. David tilted his head back, allowing the blood from the meat to drip into his mouth. He gagged it down and coughed. He was still unable to harness his abilities and process the thought of ingesting the substance, despite his body craving it so much. Using small amounts like this was just enough to keep him alive until he could better figure out what to do for himself.

"Oh God," Christian said, startling this unknown boy who locked eyes with him like a scared rat.

Christian hesitated but put out his hand and walked forward. "Hey, come here. Are you okay? Let me help you."

As he got closer, David crept further away with the meat, protecting his meal.

"It's okay. Really." Christian put the wood down. "We'll go get some help. You look like you're hurt."

David snarled at him and swiped at his hand, sending Christian several steps back as David dropped the package and sloppily ran off into the dark. Christian started to chase him, concerned for the teenage boy, but Blackheart's trio of dogs stopped him. With nothing to defend himself, he stood still as the animals sniffed in his direction and growled, the wind blowing through their dirty, tufted hair. He tried not to lock eyes with them, to not come across as aggressive. He thought of his family and backed up slowly, trying to reach the dumpster again. He heard the faint sound of a violin, which immediately caught the attention of the hounds. They all looked up, signaled by a higher power, and ran off, leaving Christian unharmed.

"What the hell was all that?" Christian asked himself, visibly shaken.

* * *

David ran through the town, doing his best to avoid the myriad of gangs, tour buses, police, and other such nighttime regulars in Meadowsville. He was still starved, only getting minimal blood from the meat packages, and couldn't focus enough to follow the sound of the violin or find any more sources of blood. It'd been days since he saw Erik die, and David had been in and out of consciousness. His waking moments had consisted of trying to feed and trying not to cry for his lost friend. He couldn't continue this way. He needed help, or he'd die.

He found refuge in a small abandoned shack among a thicket of bushes near Highway 6. On the inside wall, near the dirt floor, someone had carved AND THE NAME WE FEAR IS MR. SMITH, which was the last thing David saw before passing out again.

14

Broken Up

The next night, a middle-aged woman stood over her sleeping husband with her frizzy brown hair draped over her face. She had mild facial distortions as blood dripped down her chin in two perfect streams from the protruding canines. A rock song played in the background. Blackheart stood behind her with his hands resting on her upper arms, occasionally rubbing them firmly.

> *I'm watching all them bodies just dancing*
> *And then the music started to slow*

"I'm so thirsty," she told him calmly.

He slid his hands down to her hips, slowly and slightly rocking them back and forth, almost dancing with her to the music, against her will.

"What are you willing to do for it?" he whispered into her ear.

"I don't know."

"How bad do you want it?" he asked her, lightly tugging at her hair, having a very strong hold over her.

"Real bad," she responded sensually.

He cut his hand and let her lick it, which she did in an arousing manner.

"Do you want to be with me?"

"Yes," she said, becoming sexually excited.

"Show me." He tugged her hair harder and breathed on her neck.

This made the woman feel butterflies in her stomach, which was something that she had not felt in a long time.

She descended onto her husband, who wasn't awakened by the noise. Blackheart moved back and turned the music up, anticipating a good show. The man woke, but before he could react, his wife bit his neck and began drinking his blood with little resistance, draining him of all life. Her body started to normalize, and she fully realized what she had done.

I thought we were done forever
Not too long ago

"Oh, Jacob, I'm so sorry," she said, now holding her husband's dead body.

She walked to Blackheart with her head hung low, like a fearful child unsure of what to do. He embraced her with both arms under his pitch black coat, hugging her underneath.

"You did so well," he assured her.

"What did you do to me?"

Blackheart didn't respond but just smiled and held her harder.

"Oh, God, what have I done?" she questioned.

Blackheart tensed up when she mentioned God. "Are you sorry?" he asked.

She didn't reply.

"Would you do it again for me?"

"I don't know," she responded, completely disoriented.

His embrace intensified, and she began to feel pain from it.

"You're hurting me," she told him, unable to break his grip.

You broke that mold
And you can't be made again

He quickly grabbed her by the hair, exposed his frightening teeth, and forcibly pulled her head to one side, cutting her neck wide open with his claws. Before any blood was lost, he grabbed the wound and held it shut as she choked, spitting up blood. He kissed her with an open mouth, sucking the blood from her mouth with several fulfilling gulps, content with the blood of both victims in one action. He continued to hold the now limp corpse, slow dancing, before kissing her forehead and dropping the body. He turned up the music to full volume and left the home, fully appreciating the lyrics as they accentuated the carnage for him.

PRETERNATURAL

She'll forget who you are
Once you walk out that door
And now we're broken up

15

Farewell

David watched a memorial service, from the shadow of a large tree, for both Erik and himself. He was quite a distance from the actual ceremony but could see clearly with his new visual acuity. He was so weakened from not adequately feeding that he barely had the energy to stand upright. It was somewhat of a miracle that he was able to get to the funeral.

Several more days had passed, and it had been a tremendous struggle for him just to survive. He had taken note that being in the sunlight did not hurt him but rather seemed to just weaken him further. His enhanced senses were not able to tolerate the brightness, so it irritated his eyes and skin.

His parents, friends, classmates, and random family members were all extremely upset as they mourned openly with one another. Any question of David's parents loving him was now answered. His father was not able to look up as the occasional tear fell down his old, haggard suit. His mother was keeping to herself. She held back her tears, and her pale, freckled face was now beet red. David watched them, feeling more love for them than he could remember. The sight of what life would be after his death was gut-wrenching.

He saw Erik's parents and began to cry again. As if he were crying hard enough for the entire group. He had not cried this much ever in his life. He fought the urge to go over and explain what happened but was terrified that he would end up hurting them even more than he already had. He didn't think anyone would believe him. He might be condemned, teased, or possibly even accused of killing Erik. He couldn't risk it until he figured out what was happening to him and what his options were. His desperation was fully transparent.

David wiped his eyes and saw another large shadow suddenly standing over him among the tree branches. He turned to see Blackheart staring down at him with great empathy. It was the first time David had seen him clearly, aside from their initial meeting when he was a toddler. Blackheart's piercing sky blue eyes were mesmerizing, and his jet-black hair flowed with the wind and accompanied his long black coat. He wore meticulous formal wear under the jacket. His entire wardrobe and appearance were somehow intimidating yet hypnotic.

"Please help me," David beseeched. "I'm dying."

Blackheart looked away toward David's parents and then to him. "Do you know who I am?"

"Yes, you're the one everyone talks about. The one they're all afraid of," David said in awe.

"And you?" Blackheart asked curiously.

"If you wanted me dead, I wouldn't be here."

Blackheart nodded and smiled at David's conclusion. "David, I've watched over you for a long time. Such potential but no direction. We're going to fix that."

"Please help," he said, fading in and out of consciousness.

"You're going to pass out now. When you wake up, things will begin to make sense," Blackheart said.

He patted David's head gently, like a pet, and watched as his eyes closed and he slumped down against the tree.

David woke up much later that evening, well past curfew, in his parent's dining room. He looked around, hoping that all of the recent incidents were just a bad dream, but he then saw Blackheart. One of his father's favorite old songs began to play from the stereo as Blackheart turned it on, and the lyrics played out loudly as the scene unfolded.

You've traveled every road and reached the end
And now it's time to take my lead

"David they're going to be awake soon," Blackheart said passively.

"What is this? Why are we here?" David asked in a panic.

"This is the end of what you were and the start of what you are to become."

Your regrets are now lost in time
you did what you had to

He made a tightly clenched fist, cutting his own palm and shoving his bloody paw into David's face. David felt more able once again. He stood up, and the wounds from his battle with Erik healed quickly. He licked some of Blackheart's delicious blood off his lips. It was much different than Erik's and the deer's. It was much more potent.

"That's it. Feel it. Let it direct you," Blackheart encouraged David, smiling. "It's just enough so that you can do this."

"Do what?" David asked.

The sound of David's parents rousing made the ceiling above them creak.

"Who's there?" David's father called down.

David's body shifted toward the staircase to go meet his father, but he resisted it with all his might. He dropped to his knees and told himself to stop. Blackheart watched then grabbed his hair and began to speak to David sternly. "You disappoint me, but we'll work on it. For now, watch and learn," Blackheart proclaimed, as the music continued to play.

You've had your share of loss
Now it's time to win

Blackheart took his ghoulish claws and performed a clean, deep cut across both of David's rear thighs, immobilizing him. David winced and slammed face first onto the ground. David's father walked downstairs and saw his son. He was shocked but then looked to the now monstrous Blackheart, who quickly gored him through the stomach with a single blow.

David yelped at the scene but was muffled as his father's body was then thrown down onto him. He struggled to move but was still too weak. The blood from his father's torn midsection dripped into his mouth, and despite not wanting it, his body craved it. He took in the blood instinctually and felt empowered, which superseded his emotions.

"Taste it, David. This is your life now," Blackheart encouraged.

It's time for the winds of change
And you'd better be ready

"Mom, run!" David called to his mother.

"David, is that you?" she responded.

David managed to push his father's body off, sending it to the floor with a thud. David felt nauseous seeing him dead. He gagged and quickly noticed Blackheart had already gone to meet his mother upstairs. David pulled himself up, struggling immensely, and crawled up the stairs toward his parents' bedroom, where he found his mother's dead body being cradled like a trophy. Blackheart whispered something very subtly into her ear.

"Oh, Mom, no. Why are you doing this? I'll kill you," David screamed, running at Blackheart, who gently tossed his mother onto the king-sized bed.

David punched, bit, and kicked as hard as he could, but Blackheart stood still, not even blinking at the attacks. He grabbed David by the throat with one hand and squeezed until David passed out again. He slung David over one shoulder and walked out of the house with him, before the police arrived . . . well after the neighbors called about the loud music playing so late.

16

Nightmare

David tossed around in the midst of a vivid, colorful dream—

He stood before Blackheart, watching as he simulated their first meeting years ago, cutting his arm and licking it with a long, serpentine-like tongue. There was a bright light over his head and a darkness with fluid shadows surrounding Blackheart.

David looked down at his arm being bloodied in the same location, dripping onto the slain bodies of Erik and his parents. Their bloodied faces were imprinted on his psyche forever. He screamed as his wound began to gush like a faucet, covering the bodies and filling the space around him like a pool. He looked to Blackheart, who had taken the form of a horrifying dragon-like monster, extending his gnarled hand to him. Out of pure desperation, he took the aid and was pulled from the blood and under Blackheart's signature coat. He saw no more colors but rather just darkness.

He heard a violin playing and woke up.

Blackheart stood across the room from David, playing his instrument of choice in front of a large window on the top floor of his hideout. The low-level light from the sun seemed to avoid touching him, as if afraid to shine on him. Two of Blackheart's dogs licked David's wounds while the third stood with a dead opossum in its mouth, presenting it to David. It just stared at him with blank eyes, completely still. David cautiously took it and drank the blood, not realizing the violin had stopped. The animals trotted to their master and sat submissively at his side. David had an epiphany, and everything from his childhood encounter with Blackheart flooded back into his mind.

"I remember everything now. You're Blackheart. You're not Mr. Smith," he said as the memories from his childhood flooded back into his mind.

Blackheart nodded in agreement, acknowledging that the town called him by a false name.

"Where am I?"

"Your new home."

David looked around at his surroundings. He recognized the large mansion. "Holy shit, this is the house up on Chrysanthemum Drive I can't believe it's all true," he said with bright, starstruck eyes.

They stood in silence.

"Why am I here? Why did you do this to me?"

"I saved you."

"You killed them all. Everyone I had."

"Were they really that important to you?"

"That's an awful question," David said defensively.

"When was the last time either of your parents said they loved you? Why did your mom lock you in that basement so many times? And your father destroy the house, starve you, and push you around when he was drunk? Mom just sat there and let it happen. Fact is . . . they didn't love you."

"That's not right . . ." David responded, not having an answer. "They did love me. I understand that now, but . . ."

"And then Erik tried to kill you. He didn't even try to stop himself."

"Neither of us could control ourselves. We were both in the wrong." David paused, trying to formulate another coherent thought.

"Like it or not, I saved you," Blackheart told David.

"No, you didn't. They all cared about me. Even if they didn't say it. They all did."

"At their convenience, I'm afraid," Blackheart corrected.

"You're out of line. That's not fair to them."

"What is fair, exactly? Letting you whither and suffer like that, for all those years, just waiting for you to do something hasty like take your own life?" Blackheart paced around slowly as the dogs stayed in place, their heads following him in unison.

"The three of them knew you were having a hard time. Did any of them do anything about it to help you? Or your teachers? Or your pastor? Anyone in your life?"

David opened his mouth to talk but couldn't find the right words. Blackheart neared David and sat down next to him.

"I sat around for a decade watching you. I tried to help but could only do so much. But all those horrible people, they all held you down and kept you there. Over time, you lost yourself in it all. No hope, no faith, no anything. You met your end point."

"This isn't okay. I would've been better off dead. I can't be like this."

"For someone who still claims to believe in God, you certainly don't respect His rules."

"I don't know what to believe anymore," David responded.

"Believe that you are here with me. Believe that I am here for you."

"Why me?"

"Maybe you remind me of someone. Someone I couldn't save a long time ago. And I promised myself that I'd never let that happen again," Blackheart said in an oddly nostalgic way.

"What was their name? What happened?"

"Timothy. . ." Blackheart said under his breath, just as he did when he first met David. But he quickly dismissed the obviously important person from his past and refocused on David.

David took a distressing breath, completely unsure of what to do with himself.

"This isn't about him though. This is all for you, David. This is your chance to start over. To be better. No pain, no sickness, no limits. Let me teach you and help you achieve greatness."

David stood up, staying quiet, and looked out the window at the sun as a dark storm cloud began to cover up its brightness. It moved at the same speed as David's willingness to agree with Blackheart.

"You can say no. However, keep in mind that if you're not with me, you're just competition out there. You'll be no safer than anyone else in this town," Blackheart said in a mildly aggressive tone, growing impatient.

David looked at the cloud and stayed deep in thought for a moment. He thought of all the time he wished for something more—maybe his chance to change himself. Not in the way he had hoped, but it was something like he could never imagine.

He looked down at his arms and legs, at all of the cuts and scars from his self-harm that had begun to diminish since he transitioned into this new life. It was as if they were disappearing, along with everyone and everything he once knew, giving him a clean slate to start anew. Whether for worse or better, he was willing to take the risk. He now had no one left but Blackheart, who could guide him in this lifestyle and teach him how to control his enhanced capabilities. He had no choice but to trust himself with this person and have total faith in him.

"Okay," David agreed, feeling sick to his stomach.

17

Neglect

Christian scanned through digital articles on his desktop computer, all about Meadowsville lore, namely Mr. Smith. The events at the Meadowsville Market now had him very curious about the creatures that he encountered. Living in town his entire life, and witnessing the creature killing his parents, he'd always known there were strange things happening every day but just never had the motivation to study up on it until now.

He found minimal news reports online of associated homicides or incidents, and even the sightings were mostly blurred pictures taken by high schoolers and tourists, most of which appeared to be staged. The only thing that could always be seen clearly was a long black coat. Interviews with tourists and Meadowsville residents were contradictory to each other, and past and present township administrations' comments barely acknowledged the issues at hand. Mayor Wilkins had never said Mr. Smith's name.

As he continued to go back to the town's origin, over one hundred years past, he took note of the distinct changes of Mr. Smith's body shape and activity levels in the town compared to more recent reports.

"Is it the same person?" he asked himself, seeing distinct differences in some of the pictures.

Originally, Mr. Smith was thought to abduct children who were not respectful to his legend and make them his undead slaves. There was also suspicion of pedophilia, which could never be proven, as the missing children were never recovered, but it was strongly suspected. As time went on, children would all be taught in kindergarten how to pray at night to ward him off, but it was still not a guarantee they'd be spared. Beyond that, the legend was never explored further in advanced grades.

"Things were being covered up selectively, but why?" Christian asked himself, becoming completely focused on the inner workings of the town he'd spent his whole life in. "What is going on here?"

Mr. Smith also had been linked with several hellhounds that had been thought to assist him in his dealings. There were no pictures of the hounds, just recordings of their howls and some poor drawings from supposed witnesses. Christian, having now encountered them, got a chill down his spine thinking about it.

Mr. Smith was most frequently seen at night and was thought to live in the large, abandoned house on Chrysanthemum Drive, purposely leaving it in poor condition so no one could trace where he resided at any given time.

He was no different than any other urban legend, but the number of reports and sightings were far greater than any other out there. Tourists flocked to the town to catch a glimpse of him. He had also been extremely active in the last handful of years too. The fan-based message boards that Christian reviewed all tried to make claims that he was various types of demons, ghosts, etc., but there was no concrete basis for anything.

Adam and Caroline cried a few rooms away, neither listening to Rebecca.

"Hello? Dad? Is there a father figure in the house?" she yelled to him.

Christian smirked, ignoring the sarcastic call by his wife, knowing he should be more present for his family, but he was frozen in his ways. He continued reading deeper into the town's history. The entire marketing campaign for Mr. Smith started when Mayor Wilkins was elected several terms ago. Some conspiracy theorists proposed that she covered up the crimes in the city in order to guarantee herself reelection as she promoted the town as the safest it'd ever been under her rule. He noticed that each time her popularity dipped, there was a clear downward trend of Mr. Smith-related incidents. The township department heads were also supposedly bribed to help Wilkins manipulate the statistics in her favor. They were all in compliance, in order to keep their high-paying positions, and all of the town's staff members were all sworn to secrecy, as they each assisted in enabling Meadowsville's terrible habits.

He bypassed those pages, not believing it despite their likelihood. He came across the earliest set of pictures of Mr. Smith, which appeared to be legitimate. It was a much older man with a receding hairline and ghostly white skin, smiling right at the camera in a very unnerving way. Christian also noticed that there was a secondary, smaller shadow behind him, but the records made no reference to it. Christian wondered whether that was one of his child victims or just a coincidence.

"Christian," Rebecca yelled.

Christian read of the more recent victim's parents, who were quoted as saying Mr. Smith must have a "cold, black heart." Not known to Christian, this was where Blackheart adopted his name.

"God dammit, Christian. I need you," his wife yelled again.

He snapped out of his trance and ran to his wife, knowing full well he should've been there to help several minutes prior. He tried to apologize but also didn't appreciate her yelling and cursing at him, despite her frustration. Pure exhaustion, once again, made each of them choose poor decisions toward one another.

"Okay, all bunnies and people under four feet tall, it's time for bed," Christian called out playfully.

Caroline hopped to him and looked up, trying to wiggle her nose but failed in the most loveable way possible. Christian smiled and picked her up. She bopped her head around, putting her curly red hair into Christian's mouth, making him spit it out.

"Honey, you can't do this to your poor mother. She's too old to keep up with you," he said, winking at his wife, trying to lighten to mood.

"You're a real asshole sometimes, you know that," Rebecca said, laughing, as she carried Adam into his room.

Christian and Caroline made exaggerated shocked faces at each other.

"Mommy cursed," Caroline said.

"Yes, she did. I'm as surprised as you are," Christian responded.

He brought Caroline into her room and tucked her into bed, turning on her white noise machine and nightlight.

"Get some sleep, my little darling," he said, hugging her and kissing her forehead.

She responded with a wet, sloppy kiss on his cheek before he could stand up.

"I love you, baby."

"I love you, too, Daddy."

As Christian left the room, turning her overhead light off, he heard her begin to pray.

God almighty, who lives above,
Hear my prayers and feel my love.
Please keep me safe until day's light . . .

He came back into the room, exclaiming, "Honey, we don't do that in this house. Mr. Smith isn't real. Who taught you that, anyway?"

"The kids at school say it keeps us safe from him."

"That's not true at all. Do you really believe in him?"

"Yeah, I think so. Do you, Daddy?"

"No," he said dishonestly. "And Daddy will always be here to protect you. So there's no need to worry about anything."

She gave him a big hug and rolled over, hugging a pile of stuffed animals.

"Now, get some sleep. You have a big day of terrorizing your teachers at preschool tomorrow," he said, smiling.

Christian walked past Adam's room. His son kicked his little feet, quietly watching the little stuffed animals hanging from his crib mobile. Christian then entered his bedroom, followed by Rebecca, who had her hands full of laundry.

She dropped it on the bed and sighed. "There's got to be a better way than this," she said.

"If you find it, please let me know," Christian said, hugging her from behind.

She stood up, enjoying his embrace.

"What do we do now?" he asked, partially testing the waters to see if she would be interested in sex again.

"Sleep sounds nice," she said as they let go of each other.

"You sure that's it?" Christian said, looking at the bed slyly.

Rebecca tilted her head, giving him a look of obvious rejection. "If you help me with this giant pile of laundry and we're both still standing, it's a deal," she baited.

Christian ground his teeth and shoved all the laundry off the bed. "Yeah, you're right. Let's go to bed," he responded, not even attempting to negotiate with her. "I'll just give it to you twice as hard tomorrow."

"And twice as fast, I'm sure" she said, extinguishing his confidence jokingly.

Rebecca giggled and told him he was cute and she'd be ready for it. They had a pleasant kiss before they changed into their night wear and adjourned to the bed, both extremely tired. They held hands as until Rebecca fell asleep. Christian stayed awake, thinking about his research.

18

Breakdown

Blackheart and David spent much time together over the next few weeks. David still struggled to kill, which exasperated his mentor. He brought David to a seemingly specific house one night, and they broke through the back door.

"You need to become very comfortable with this. It's already been too long," he told David. He began thumbing through some loose CDs near the stereo system in the living room. "Your safety depends on it. And so does your survival."

"I try, but it's too hard," David said, repeating his struggles to Blackheart continuously.

Blackheart delicately put on a very peppy song that was reflective of their interaction.

I was hanging around feeling sorry for myself
you're just not getting me at all

"Why do you play music?" David inquired.

"It's an old pastime of mine. It heightens the experience for me," Blackheart said with his eyes shut, listening to the song. "But the song has to be just right."

David became uncomfortable, knowing that not only did Blackheart see no issue with killing but he strived to enjoy it as much as possible. As he went to nervously ask more questions, to delay the inevitable kill, Blackheart began to transform into his more hideous state.

"Are you ready?" Blackheart asked in a gnarled voice, hoping to finally hear David become excited to kill.

"Yes . . ." David said. He was very unsure of himself, and it came across clearly.

Blackheart tried another method to get through to David. "Are you thirsty?"

"Yes . . ." David said reluctantly.

"Then kill," he commanded, shoving David toward the bedroom.

I know it's my call
But I ain't ready for the big time yet

An older couple was sleeping but beginning to rouse due to the noise from the music playing. David walked to the woman but was quickly redirected to the man by Blackheart.

"Leave her for me," he instructed.

David grabbed the old man and threw him onto the floor, turning himself into his altered form. As his teeth began to grow, the blood from his gums initiated the change in his body. He bit the man's neck and began to drink the blood, trying to ignore the screams. He continued to feed but couldn't get past the cries of his victim. Blackheart held the woman. She screamed and tried to get away from him as he became increasingly hostile at David's faltering. David stopped, letting the man go, and froze like a deer in headlights.

Blackheart covered the woman's mouth and accidentally crushed her entire skull out of frustration. The man held his hemorrhaging neck and screamed out the one open window for help. Several neighbors heard the commotion and shut their windows to ignore it.

"What're you doing?" Blackheart yelled at David furiously.

"I'm sorry . . ." he replied, throwing his hands up, hoping to not disappoint Blackheart again. "I just can't do it. I'm sorry."

I missed a lot of good stuff
But I gotta keep true to me

Blackheart stared David down, and without looking, he grabbed the old man with a single hand. He severed his throat, squirting blood all over David, disorienting his protégé.

If you take this from me
I don't know where I'd be

He put a hand on David's shoulder and threw him out the open window and onto the street. David tried to stand, but before he could, Blackheart grabbed his arm and leapt into the sky, holding him like a toy. David didn't know what direction he was being taken or what was happening. He yelled for Blackheart to stop, which he refused to do.

"Feast or famine. You're on your own," Blackheart told David, unexpectedly dropping him straight down onto White Tulip Avenue.

David stood and looked for Blackheart, who had vanished. Extreme anger and thirst combated one another for David's attention, and he began to relinquish control again. He let out a very loud roar only to see one light come on, with Christian's daughter, Caroline, looking out the window of her bedroom.

David jumped up to her room, breaking through the wall, and grabbed the girl. She was frightened as she saw his hideous face. David floated back and forth between laughing and crying. Adam began to scream from down the hall as all the commotion woke him.

"Caroline," Rebecca screamed, running toward the room.

David kicked the door shut, slamming Rebecca in the face, knocking her out and injuring her badly. He jumped outside with his victim and saw his reflection in a nearby car window, which made him even more upset and unstable. He had become something much worse than he ever imagined.

Christian pulled onto the road on his way home from work and saw the commotion. He sped up and jumped out of the car, seeing the backside of David. He slowly turned, displaying

Caroline's limp little body in his arms. Blood covered her pajamas, and no sign of life was in his daughter.

"I'm so sorry," David said to Christian, realizing the full extent of his first kill.

Christian ran at David, screaming. David dropped the girl and fled. Christian tackled him, but David kicked him viciously, sending him into the side of his car and knocking him out.

David jumped for what seemed like an eternity, feeling the sprinkles of an incoming rain storm. The sounds of Adam crying didn't diminish, no matter how far David got from the scene. He screamed in anger at himself, cutting at his body, until a bolt of lightning struck a satellite dish next to him, atop one house. He was distracted and accidentally fell against a chimney, breaking it into hundreds of pieces, and proceeded to crash into various other structures, due to the immense speed he was traveling.

He ended up landing near a church that he had never seen before on Daffodil Drive named Meadowsville Community Church. He looked at the cross on top of the building, feeling the rain start to come down abundantly, washing all of the blood and dirt off his body. He stood there, hoping to be washed of his sins and saved.

The large front doors of the church swung slightly open as he looked into the enlightened entrance. Something deep inside his stomach called for him to enter, which he did. The inside was covered in aged wood, which was in very good shape for an older building. A light red rug led him from the entranceway toward the altar, which showed an overwhelmingly large stained glass window above it, depicting Jesus looking down. David went to the front of the altar and dropped to his knees. With nothing left to lose, he began to speak openly, hoping God finally heard him.

He started tearing up again. "I asked You for help so many times. This is what I am now due to Your absence. Why have You let this be done to me?"

The silence was deafening, and David's soul ached at his assumed negligence of the Lord.

"I want an answer! I want it now, God dammit! Answer me!"

David broke down crying, hearing nothing else but the continued quiet of the church. As he sobbed for several minutes, he felt a hand on his back. He flinched and fell over, not hearing anyone approach him. A stout priest looked down at him with kind, welcoming eyes, and there was a young girl behind him. Both looked at David inquisitively until the priest finally spoke.

"Oh my goodness, why are you crying?" he asked with sincere concern.

David tried to respond but was weeping too hard.

"It's okay, you're safe here. We don't have to talk now," he said, keeping his hand on David's back.

David cried in the arms of the priest, harder than he ever had before, almost atoning for every sin he'd ever committed.

19

Aftermath

Christian awoke to paramedics assessing him.

"Mr. Reed, can you hear me?" one of the first responders asked, shining a light in his eyes.

Despite his disoriented feelings and slightly blurred vision, Christian could see her lips moving, but he didn't hear a single thing. He looked around to see his wife with bandaging all over her battered face, crying hysterically as she was being stretchered into an ambulance.

"Let's get him in the ambulance and over to the hospital," another worker said, beginning to strap Christian to the stretcher.

He then managed to push them off and stand on his own power. He stumbled over to Rebecca and shoved the first responders off of her in the back of the ambulance.

She kept mouthing, "Our baby is gone" over and over again, referencing Caroline. She couldn't stop herself from saying it repeatedly. With the loss of Caroline, on top of all the stress she and Christian faced on a daily basis, she had completely broken down.

Christian looked behind him at the side of the house, seeing the large hole from the attack and Caroline covered up on the ground. One of the officers was speaking to his superiors on scene, pointing up to the sky, as if telling him this was an accident from the lightning during the earlier rainstorm. Several neighbors were arguing with each other about what happened as officers attempted to calm their tensions.

Chief Jones arrived on scene, looking at the damage, and began explaining to the responding officers how to type up the report to make it look like an accident and not an incident. He looked at Christian then averted his eyes, as he understood the injustice done here. But he was powerless to go against Mayor Wilkins's orders. She would have him fired and replaced immediately if something like this was made public. Seeing Caroline's body shook Jones to his core. Things were no longer quiet, as they used to be. The town was losing control of its unique problem.

Christian's stomach ached, and his abdomen tightened as he began to remember everything that happened. He kissed Rebecca and fell out of the ambulance, crawling to Caroline's body. He put his head gently on top of her, crying and screaming, feeling complete responsibility for her death.

"Daddy will always be here to protect you," he recalled telling her, which had now been degraded into a lie.

He screamed at the top of his lungs. His sense of hearing returned. A small group of police tried to pull him away, but he resisted and began fighting them off violently. He punched several of the officers, not caring about the pain in his hands from each hit.

"I was supposed to protect her! I was supposed to protect her," he screamed between cries as they restrained him.

"Sir, you need to calm down. She's gone. We're sorry, but it's too late," one of the officers said, holding Christian's arms down.

Christian was handcuffed and put in the back of a patrol car. Chief Jones looked on, realizing that he had been the first responder to the call of the night when Christian's parents were killed. He remembered seeing Christian as a five-year-old, completely broken after witnessing the death of his parents. Now, as a thirty-five-year-old, he saw him experiencing the same type of trauma once again. A few tears fell down his face, and he quickly wiped them off to proceed with helping his officers on the scene, struggling with his feelings on the situation.

Christian watched as Adam was carried off by an officer, his wife was closed up in the ambulance, and Caroline was taken away in a body bag. His entire family fractured in front of him. He should have been home to protect them. He struggled in the car, screaming and trying to get himself free, but his attempts were fruitless.

20

Newsworthy

Days passed, and the Meadowsville local news aired a report.

A well-endowed, provocatively dressed young girl appeared on screen, smiling. "Welcome to the Wednesday edition of Channel 1, Meadowsville's best source for your news. I'm Debbie Johnson with your local updates.

"A vicious lightning storm is still the talk of the area, as several properties were reported damaged and several homes are still without power . . ."

Several homes, including Christian's, were quickly shown in the background.

"The Meadowsville Maulers football team will take on the Totensville Titans at home tomorrow night. Will they be able to defend their home turf and maintain their almost perfect season? Go home team!

"Several teens from Meadowsville High are doing their part by scrubbing Mr. Smith graffiti off several local businesses . . ."

Students were shown cleaning the locker rooms in Meadowsville High School as Mayor Wilkins posed for photos with them, sporting an obviously fake smile.

"Speaking of our own local legend, we have our weekly viewer sighting by Jermaine Meyers, a visiting photographer all the way from Colorado . . ."

An unfocused, authentic picture of Blackheart perched on a building was displayed behind her.

"Stay on the lookout at all times because you never know when Mr. Smith is watching. Be sure to send in your pictures for a chance to win our monthly prize drawings.

"That's your local update. Be safe and remember to be home by curfew. This is Debbie Johnson."

21

Rebuilding

Christian sat in his home alone, bandaged up and enjoying total darkness around him. He was beyond reason and felt nothing but rage. A breeze from the damaged upstairs greeted him every so often. The streetlight exposed several family pictures on the mantle of the fireplace. A small shadow was cast over a recent picture of the family, blocking out Caroline, showing Christian his new family unit for the first time. He breathed deeply, almost letting out a growl with each exhalation.

He thought back to his visit earlier that day with Rebecca in the Meadowsville Medical Center. Her face was still heavily distressed, even several days after the attack. Aside from a severe concussion, David's attack yielded a broken nose and orbital bone, mild hearing loss, and a fractured jaw. She would be a patient at the facility for at least several weeks.

"Where is Adam?" Christian asked.

"He's with my parents," Rebecca muttered hesitantly.

"Oh no. That can't be," Christian said, feeling sick about it.

"They had no choice for right now. It's temporary. I hate the fact that I had to ask them. We'll get him back soon enough. I feel like I failed our family. I should've done more to save her," she told her husband.

They both started to tear up, and they put their foreheads together, each hoping the other would remain an emotional crutch, as they had grown accustomed to. But the mood was different now. Both Rebecca and Christian were in a very deep depression after the death of Caroline and now questioned how to be proper parents to Adam.

"I miss her so much," she said.

"I know. I know. I do too. I was supposed to protect her," Christian said, fighting back tears.

They stayed silent and held each other.

"How did this happen? What was that thing?" she asked Christian.

"I don't know. But I should've been home. I was supposed to be there," he admitted, feeling guilty but unable to utter an apology, which frustrated him even more.

"It's nothing you could have prevented. Don't do that to yourself."

"I'm going to fix all this. I promise you. I will make this right," he promised her.

"Please don't do anything rash. Adam and I need you more than ever now. We need to be there for each other," she pleaded as Christian stood up.

"I know." He kissed her, not sure of his intentions yet, and started to leave the hospital room.

"Please be careful. I love you."

Christian stopped at the doorway. "I love you too." But he didn't turn around.

Rebecca had always been his source of stability, and now she was unable to accommodate him. His mindset began to shift to a dangerous place.

Christian came out of his memory and saw a small macaroni-based necklace that Caroline made for him hanging on the coatrack across the room. He gently picked it up and examined it while missing his daughter terribly. Blackheart's dogs howled, and he ran outside the house, hoping he encountered one of them. He wanted to hurt something and didn't care what it was. He grabbed his ax to defend himself, but much to his disappointment, there was nothing present to combat him. He yelled as loud as he could, silencing the howls and shaking the windows of his neighbors, who didn't look out at the disturbance. Christian now knew what he must do. He had finally found his calling. He was ready to save this town from the atrocities that had existed for too long.

He walked back into the house, tossing the ax down. He laced up a worn pair of sneakers, drew on his favorite brown trench coat, and put Caroline's necklace on so it rested on top of the silver cross that he always wore. A new energy filled his body, and he was prepared for what he must do.

"God, give me strength," he said, leaving the house and going into the night.

* * *

Across town, David remained in the church, speaking with Father Richard. His daughter, Alexandra, stayed mostly quiet, as she was uncomfortable with David's presence. They had had private disagreements about taking David in, which they had opposing views on. Alexandra, about to begin training to become a priest, was more judgmental toward David, whereas her father was more accepting. Father Richard explained to her that as she furthered her education over the years, she would understand his position toward David much better. He made the ruling that David would be allowed to stay with them. While resentful about it, she appreciated her father's mindset and focused her efforts on trying to understand it and not being so critical. This would play a key role in her professional development as a future spiritual leader for a congregation.

David had explained his unique situation to Father Richard, who surprisingly listened to him without condemnation of any kind. David had unloaded on his new allies, who had tried their best to understand his position and provide the guidance he needed.

"Thank you for taking care of me these past few days," David expressed to both.

"It was no problem," Father Richard responded.

"I don't know where to go from here. I don't know what to do. I can't trust Blackheart. He took everything from me. I can't go back there," David said, sniffling a bit.

Father Richard patted his shoulder. "You're stronger than you think. And God will keep watch over you no matter what."

"I have my doubts about that sometimes. He's been absent for a long time. Like He forgot about me."

Father Richard felt strong empathy toward the struggling youth and replied, "David, remember that He loves you. He'll always love you. Unconditionally. No matter how hard you hate Him."

"But why all this? Why does He keep hurting me?"

"You just have to trust in his decisions. Blind faith is very hard. Just because things seem terrible or don't go according to how someone thinks they should, or even when they are expected to . . . you have to use those times to keep your faith strong. He's by your side for all of it. He is all-knowing and will always make sure things happen exactly as they need to. The universe will always balance itself out because He keeps it that way. What we perceive as 'good' and 'bad' both have their places in this world but always balance each other out."

"But I've killed now. I may be beyond His reach."

"I can't speak for Him, but I think I have a pretty good understanding of His word. It's not my job to judge or denounce anyone or anything. That's above my pay grade. That's for my boss to do. His love always seems to overwhelm judgment for any sin that you are truly sorry for committing," Father Richard said, sporting a very comforting smile.

Alexandra, who continued to stay silent, closed her eyes and nodded in agreement with her father. Her struggle with the entire situation did not improve, but she tried to stay an active participant in the discussion, hoping to learn valuable lessons. She was also four years older than David and wasn't sure what to casually speak with him about.

"Are you hungry?" she blurted out, trying to find anything to say.

"Yes," David responded, unable to look at her due to his anxiety with women.

He looked at her gorgeous green eyes and became nervous but observed that she was uncomfortable too.

"I think we have some extra oven roasters in the fridge. Let me go put something together," Father Richard added, purposely leaving the two together so his daughter could practice her inadequate communication skills with David.

Both Alexandra and David sat in silence, not looking at each other much. David was further irritated that even with his new abilities, his anxiety was still as strong as ever. He looked up at her again, nervously fiddling with his hands, as neither was able to find anything to talk about.

"I'm sorry. I'm not really good at this, Alexandra," he admitted to her.

"At what?"

"Talking to girls," David said, fully relaying his shyness to her.

"You're doing just fine," she said, winking at him, hoping to make him a little more comfortable. "And please, call me Alex."

David smiled and looked down to the floor. He saw a drop of blood from his attack on Caroline and recalled what her little body felt like when he killed her. He sighed loudly and looked to the stained glass window over the altar, observing Jesus looking down at him.

Alexandra collected her thoughts and began to understand David's position more clearly. "I'm sorry for all your losses. We lost my mom a few years back. It hurts for a long time. You'll never really get over it, but it gets a little easier as time goes on. I know you've had more than that, but you're in good company here with us. And of course Him," she said, looking up at Jesus.

She met David's view of the window.

"Thank you," he said sincerely.

They became quiet again. But they stayed with one another, and the conversation became more inquisitive as Alex yearned to better understand David's condition.

"What's it feel like?"

"What?"

"When you start to turn?"

"It's uncomfortable."

"Describe it for me," she pried with the utmost curiosity.

"Um . . . okay. Imagine how your body feels right after you sprint as fast as you can. Your heart pounds, you sweat, and your entire body feels like it's invincible. That, but the pumped-up feeling keeps going and doesn't stop. Your body grows and changes, and you feel like a prisoner inside this monster, with little to no control. And you can only think about doing whatever it takes to appease it."

"Is it like a disease?"

"I'm not sure. I never got to ask a lot of questions. I'm not really sure anyone knows."

"Do you have to get bitten?"

"I think it can be any type of bodily fluids transmitted," he replied, not realizing that he unexpectedly made a sexual reference to Alex.

"That doesn't sound too appealing." She chuckled.

David smiled at her as their identical green gazes met.

"I don't mean to stay quiet when you're with my dad. I just feel like you and he need a lot of time to talk."

"He's a good man."

"You have no idea," she replied. "He's very strong. I can only hope to be as good as him one day."

Alexandra fully displayed her meager and meek demeanor, but David felt her sincerity. He understood her potential as much as her father did.

"So you want to become a priest?"

"I do," she replied, nonverbally expressing some indecisiveness on her future. "Seems like it's kind of expected of me, you know? I don't really know anything else beyond this."

David appreciated her honesty and nodded.

"Kids, come on!" Father Richard yelled from down the hall.

David and Alexandra walked together. David tried not to stare, but he was attracted to Alex, despite knowing that they could never have anything beyond a friendship. Between her being older than him and his predicament, it was just a sad case of bad circumstances. He realized at this point how he was able to bypass his anxiety to engage her. He smiled briefly to himself, feeling accomplished. Alexandra had similar feelings but also understood the situation as he did. Most people disregarded her in favor of Father Richard, but David was the first person to give her their undivided attention.

They sat at a small table that Father Richard had prepared. David had a bowl of chicken blood, and two plates of reheated chicken and vegetables were placed for Father Richard and Alex. They all watched each other, waiting for someone to eat.

"This feels funny," David said. "I can do this in another room if it grosses you out."

"Think nothing of it," Richard responded. "We all need sustenance . . . it's just a little different in your case." He smiled, making both Alex and David feel more at ease.

"Dad, I've seen you eat plenty of weirder stuff than that," Alex said to her dad, trying to ride his momentum to lighten the mood.

"Waste not, want not, right," he joked back.

All three giggled and enjoyed each other's company. None of them had had a sit-down meal like that in a long time. David, never knowing this type of positive family dynamic, was fascinated.

22

Confrontation

David left the company of his newfound friends later that evening. He realized Blackheart would come looking for him eventually, and as idealistic as it would be to disappear, never having to encounter him again wasn't a viable option. He also did not want to endanger anyone else. He searched all over town, eventually finding Blackheart sitting atop a sign, high above Highway 6. Blackheart had a particular scent that resembled lavender that David was able to eventually pick up on with his increased sense of smell. David carefully climbed up to reach Blackheart as the cool autumn breeze caressed his hair.

"Nice of you to come back," Blackheart said, exposed from the mouth down by passing cars.

"You made me kill that little girl," David said angrily.

"Yes, I did. And aside from some unnecessary attention, you did well. It'll be covered up just like everything else. So don't worry about it."

"Why did you make me do that?" David asked.

"Now you won't starve. You'll just feed, like you should. No matter what, you'll be able to take a life to defend yourself, if necessary. I had to do it for your own good."

"But I could've starved to death or been found and killed. You just left me for dead."

"But you didn't. You're much too resilient. I've always known that about you. That's why you've made it this far," he responded calmly.

"How do you think it's okay to kill people like this? Animals, I understand, but people? It's not right."

"David, you've now had human blood. You know how much different it tastes. How much more satisfying it is. Sometimes, you just need to treat yourself. It's not all bad being like us."

They stayed quiet and watched several luxury cars, all belonging to the fairly wealthy town residents, drive under them.

"Have you kept anyone else around like me?" David asked.

"No."

David questioned the answer and still wondered who the Timothy was that Blackheart referenced earlier.

"Who was Timothy?"

"Someone very important to me."

"Is he still alive? Was he your son?"

Blackheart ignored the further inquiries. David stopped himself from asking anything else, out of fear of Blackheart's possible volatile response, and moved on.

"Do you believe in God?"

"I believe that there is more in this world than meets the eye. We're prime examples of that."

"What about God?"

"I think it's a nice idea for weak people."

More cars sped under them.

"David, I realize that this has all been very intense, but you're handling it well. I'm not like a human, as you've grown accustomed to. I'm here to guide you. And plan to do so for a very long time. I want to see you succeed."

There was some validity to Blackheart's responses, and what David had interpreted as abuse might have actually just been for his own good. He questioned his prior feelings about the situation, as discussed with Father Richard and Alex, and remained unsure of the position he needed to take. Blackheart might be a proficient manipulator or just a distinctive mentor. David needed more time to figure it all out.

* * *

Several miles away, the nightly Tour of Terrors bus drove along. Actors dressed in long trench coats, all wearing fake fangs, jumped out from select locations, smacking the bus and hissing. The mixed group of tourists inside the van snapped pictures and screamed, having a blast. The van continued on to view the animal carcasses that public works purposely placed in several of the graveyards around town. The actors playing Blackheart took the fangs out, high-fiving each other and laughing.

"Easiest paycheck I've ever gotten," the one actor said to another.

Christian watched from the shadows nearby, gently rubbing the top of his ax. He walked around the town, moving as a shadow, looking for any signs of the creatures, but saw nothing organic. He was careful to avoid police cars, gangs, and tour buses. He ultimately found himself at the base of Chrysanthemum Drive and looked up at Blackheart's lair.

He walked up the long dirt road, went up to the house without hesitation or fear, and kicked the front door in. The house was in complete disarray but completely still. He walked through each floor, examining the various items and broken furniture inside. After realizing that his efforts were wasted there, he went back toward the door to exit. He saw a figure blocking the way, wearing a long jacket.

His heart rate increasing rapidly, Christian grabbed his ax hard. "I'm not afraid of you. Any of you," he yelled.

The figure tried to back outside, but Christian charged, swinging his ax wildly, narrowly missing the individual each time as they stumbled out of the house together.

"Where are the others? You tell me now or you're fucking dead!" he yelled, acting irrationally.

"Please don't. I'm an actor. Don't kill me," the person cried out, covering his face, falling to the ground.

Christian put his weapon down and sneered at the man.

"I thought you were with the tour. Don't hurt me, man," the person begged.

Christian, more enraged, pulled the man off the ground, feeling stronger than normal, and shoved him away. "Get outta here now," Christian barked out, catching his breath.

The man ran away frantically, and Christian screamed again, driving the ax deep into the ground.

23

Visit

S o does anything hurt you?" Alexandra asked David
as they sat on the altar of Meadowsville Community
Church.

She handed him a cross, and he graciously accepted it
as they both looked to better understand David's condition
and its limitations.

"Yeah, it does. Just like normal. But it's blunted, and we
can recover quickly if we drink blood."

Both waited momentarily for the cross to burn David,
but nothing happened. They looked at each other with play-
ful disappointment.

"What's it taste like?"

"Tangy. Takes some getting used to," he said, making
both smile.

"Are there differences between types of blood?"

"Yeah, it's almost like when you eat a piece of fruit. Even if the same type, some taste different than others, but still all fruit. Does that make sense?"

"Sort of, yeah." She furrowed her brow. "What else can we test out?" she said, looking around eagerly. "What about holy water?"

"Let's give it a shot," David agreed, enjoying himself.

Alexandra cupped her hand into the holy water and dripped it all over his palm. They both waited to see what would happen. David closed his eyes, unsure of the potential discomfort he was facing from playing such a silly game with his new friend. But nothing happened.

"So nothing with religion?"

"The way I understood it from Blackheart . . . only if you truly believe something will harm you, or if there is a deep-seated fear of it, can it actually do so."

"So you don't fear God?" she asked, handing David a cloth to wipe off the holy water.

"No, I don't. I just wish I understood Him better."

David felt the small sensation of needing more blood but was able to control it more when he was around Alex.

"Why do you need blood? Why not actual food or something else?"

"I guess because it gets used up so quick when we turn, it's like your body goes into a wild starvation mode. You kinda need fuel for the fire. Not sure why nothing else works."

David remembered killing Caroline and looked down, upset with himself.

"David, are you okay? We don't have to do this anymore," Alex said, concerned for her only friend.

"I'm okay. I just need to get some air. I'll be back in a little bit," he said, quickly leaving.

Alex was left wondering whether she'd taken things too far. She cleaned up and went back to her studies in David's absence.

David, now harnessing his abilities increasingly each day, traveled gracefully across the town, ending up across the street of Christian's house. He looked at the hole in the side of the home, with a loose plastic cover whipping around in the wind. He didn't realize it, but Christian was inside, just beyond the reach of the streetlight, staring back at him.

Back at the church, Alex began shutting the windows and locking the doors for the night then heard a gentle knock. She opened the door, expecting David, but saw Blackheart and his hounds appearing as a most fearsome group. She had heard the stories of this feared creature; much like everyone else in town, she didn't know his true name, but was not at all prepared for him to appear in front of her. Her stomach became uneasy, and she froze, unsure of what steps to take to ensure the safety of both herself and her father.

The dogs looked at her with drool dripping down their mangled snouts, with sounds of their deep breathing patterns all playing against one another in an almost harmonious melody. Blackheart looked down at her, not breaking an intense stare. She sensed his powerful presence and walked slowly backward toward the altar.

Blackheart walked in by himself as the dogs remained outside, walking in line with him, just outside the windows. With each step Alexandra took back, Blackheart took a long stride ahead, towering over her. She accidentally backed into a pew and, before she could rebalance herself, Blackheart stood mere inches from her. She froze as he peered over her and smelled her neck. He sensed her pure innocence, and it delighted him.

"You wanna know what I love best about women? Hesitation and uncertainty. It makes them so fun to play with," he said with wandering eyes.

She ran to the altar as her father walked in toward the podium.

"Come here, dear," Father Richard called to her.

She ran behind him, looking for anything to use as a weapon, but couldn't find anything. Father Richard walked to the end of the altar, meeting their visitor, who stayed below him on the main floor in a spiritually symbolic position.

"So I understand that you two have met my friend David," Blackheart said, speaking to both Alexandra and Father Richard.

The dogs were heard, circling the outside of the church.

Blackheart looked around. "Quaint," he said sarcastically.

Father Richard stood tall.

"David is a good boy. He just has a lot to learn," Blackheart said, gliding one extended fingernail across the altar rail.

He looked past Father Richard and toward Alex with hungry eyes. "I see why David likes it here. She's very pretty," he said, sniffing the air carefully in Alexandra's direction, as if to remember her scent.

Alexandra was disgusted at his comment but was much too timid to do anything about it.

"He's asking me a lot of odd questions. I don't know what you two are filling his head with, but I'd like it to stop now."

Father Richard did not waver and replied, "David will decide what he wants to believe for himself. It is between him and God, and no one else. And that includes you."

"Then why are you trying to sway him?" Blackheart inquired.

"I'm not. Like yourself, I merely represent one end of the equation. I have total faith that He will guide David in the right direction."

Blackheart pulled his upper lip high, as if to brag about his fangs, and licked them.

"You don't intimidate me, and you won't hurt me. God will protect us, and He is stronger than you could ever hope to be." Father Richard fought back again.

"We'll see about that," Blackheart said, still smiling ear to ear.

Blackheart restrained himself due to a large secret that no one else was aware of. He very much feared God and did his best to hide it, as it could be used against him as his only potential weakness.

"Who says I'd hurt you . . . when I have much better options?" Blackheart glanced at Alexandra again. "Little girl, Daddy won't always be here to protect you."

He backed away, watching both, leaving with his dogs following close behind.

Father Richard and Alex hugged one another, both scared to death.

24

Interruption

L ater that evening, Blackheart, at the scene at his next victim, observed an older woman feasting on her elderly husband, taking great delight in it. He created these scenes and manipulated women into giving him a show before taking their lives. It was just a matter of finding their vulnerabilities and capitalizing on them. Making them think that they needed him. He appreciated all of his kills, despite the gender. He just happened to prefer women but would slaughter a man just the same. He was killing people for a specific reason. Making them pay a penance of sorts.

A slow-paced song played at a lower volume than he normally preferred it at. The woman stood up and threw her arms around Blackheart, proud of herself.

I care for you with all that I have
You lift my spirit and lighten my soul

"How was that?" he asked her.

"So great. God, I love this," she exclaimed with a gnarled face as he held her.

No one knows where I'd be
If it wasn't for you

Blackheart opened his mouth to feast on her when the back door was kicked in. Christian walked into the room looking grizzled and furious, holding his ax. He had been tracking Blackheart for the last few days but unfortunately wasn't able to stop this homicide before it happened.

"Mr. Smith, I presume?" Christian called out, wielding his ax.

Blackheart laughed hard at Christian's misquote as it echoed through the house. He stopped and took the woman by the hair, dragging her across the room, moving closer to Christian. She struggled but couldn't get free from his grasp.

"Let her go," Christian demanded.

Blackheart couldn't focus. He had never had a kill interrupted. He was intrigued by Christian's courage. He looked at his victim and back to Christian before roaring in his face and throwing the woman at him.

If I ever find you gone
I don't know what would become of me

Christian caught her and both fell, breaking the kitchen table behind them. The woman snapped her fangs in Christian's face as he held her off with the handle of his ax. After a brief struggle, he rolled her away and got to his feet. She crouched low to the ground and hissed like an intimidated animal. Christian played out several lines in his mind of how to attempt to reason with her. But he saw that she was past that point and would kill him unless he acted. She jumped at him, missing, and against his better judgment, he drove his ax through the back of her neck, killing her instantly.

Life would continue
But what would be the point

Christian was alarmed by his action and gagged multiple times, almost vomiting. This was the first time he killed, and it was worse than he'd even imagined. He spat on the ground, looking at Blackheart, now outside with several police cars shining their spotlights on him with guns raised. He roared at them, and the officers slowly lowered their weapons, each one more afraid than the next, letting Blackheart make a getaway. He jumped away from the scene in a single bound, landing out of sight. The officers entered the house, but Christian had also escaped.

25

Warning

The following day, Christian stood at Caroline's grave. He looked alarmingly unkempt but didn't care if anyone saw him. He was here for his daughter, which he couldn't do when she was still alive. He continually beat himself up for this and would do so for a very long time. He knelt down and quietly prayed for her. The small memorial service that was recently held in his wife's hospital room flowed through his mind.

"You should still be here. We miss you more than you will ever know, my baby girl," he said, holding back tears.

A cool wind blew past him, and he noticed Blackheart standing across from him. Christian stood up, and both of their trench coats glided through the breeze. They physically matched one another, and neither backed down.

"Christian," Blackheart said, walking casually toward him as if greeting an acquaintance.

"You don't scare me. I don't care what you are, Smith," Christian said, ready for battle.

"I'm truly sorry that your daughter was lost. I understand your pain. I've lost many children over the years myself." He waved his arms at an entire row of low graves for lost children, indicating that he lied to David about former protégés.

"Where is the boy?" Christian asked, concerning himself with David now. "He killed my daughter, and he deserves to die."

"David? Not sure. But despite my best instruction, he still makes mistakes. I won't stand in your way as you do whatever you need to resolve this matter with him," Blackheart said, beginning to walk away in a cocky manner.

"I won't stop with him. I'll come for you too," Christian called to him.

Blackheart stopped and walked back to Christian. He circled around him like a shark, getting closer to him as he completed each rotation.

He finally got nose-to-nose with Christian and sneered. "Take what's left of your family and let it be. Consider this my first and only warning. My name is Blackheart. You'll learn to respect it."

Blackheart walked away, leaving Christian to his thoughts for the remainder of the day. He visited his wife again that night, but she was heavily sedated in her hospital room and unaware of his presence. He left to visit Adam that night, who had been given over to Rebecca's parents temporarily. He became lost in his thoughts during his trip to their home, wondering whether the truth about Mr. Smith and Blackheart would ever be known to Meadowsville. And how far would he have to take this personal battle of his? How much more would he have to sacrifice to right all the wrongs here? Was this going to be his new calling in life?

He reached his in-laws' house, which was a twenty-minute walk from the hospital. Christian knocked on the door, queasy being in their presence and wishing they were not involved in this situation. His mother-in-law opened the door. She had on her standard stretch pants and olive green sweater and gave him a disapproving look, which he had grown numb to over the years. She criticized his appearance and odor and asked where he'd been. Christian walked past her, not dignifying her with even one word, and went upstairs to their spare bedroom to see his son. She called out to him to be a better parent and take care of Adam. She then yelled that Adam was asleep and not to wake him. Christian continued on, hearing his father-in-law watching television in another part of the house, not becoming part of the conversation, which he was content with.

The television had a breaking news story from Channel 1, concerning the disappearances of Smith's—no, Blackheart's—most recent victim. Enraged family members were causing chaos at the town hall in front of the mayor's office. One of the reporters tried to get a comment from Mayor Wilkins, who ignored the questions, retreating into her office. Then they tried to speak with Chief Jones, who started to tear up and also avoided the reporters. He was no longer able to handle the stress of his job or the corruption of his superior.

Christian opened the bedroom door and found Blackheart sitting in a rocking chair, cradling a sleeping Adam. He tensed up, unsure of what to do. Blackheart stood up and gently handed Adam to Christian, breathing into his face with sour breath, grinning. His warning was now fully understood. Christian took Adam, keeping eye contact with his tormentor, and watched as he left through the open window.

He hugged Adam and put him back into the crib, watching him sleep peacefully. He sat in the rocking chair, considering his options. Did he piece together what was left of his family and continue on, despite their loss? Did he put it all on the line to protect everyone in town forever? Was it worth the risk? He understood that neither option was ideal, but he was still faced with choosing one.

"Why won't he kill me?" he said under his breath, wondering why Blackheart seemed to resist hurting him.

26

Halloween

David feasted uncomfortably on a dead deer that was very recently killed by a car. He wasn't sure whether he should feel ashamed or proud that he still couldn't take a life with ease, as Blackheart had instructed.

It was Halloween night, and he watched the families and children running house to house, collecting huge amounts of candy before the nine o'clock curfew. Their costumes included little devils, ghosts, soldiers, and everything you could imagine, all in the name of good fun. Each home in Meadowsville was extravagantly decorated, adding to the enjoyment of such a day.

He reminisced about when he and Erik used to strategically switch parts of their costumes, hitting up the houses giving the largest candy bars multiple times. He chuckled to himself but quieted soon after. He missed his friend. David remembered his mother wrapping him in bandages when he was little, dressing him like a mummy and taking pictures with his father. It wasn't always so bad in his young life. He continued feeding, reflecting on his losses.

He hadn't spoken to Alex, Father Richard, or even Blackheart in several days. He still wasn't sure how to progress in his current state and was considering all his options, none of which seem like a good fit.

He sucked up the last bit of blood and hid the deer under a pile of leaves. As he finished, he turned and realized there was a rope tied around his foot. He attempted to remove it. Before he could do so, a car screeched, and he was pulled violently from the protection of the woods. The vehicle sped around for several minutes, dragging him along as his skin was peeled off on the pavement with each twist and turn. The car stopped, and David tried to get up but was physically unable to. He looked up to see Christian staring down at him.

"I'll never let another parent mourn like I have," he said, shoving his boot onto David's face, pushing it into the ground and making his response to Blackheart's ultimatum clear.

"Stop," David cried, recognizing Christian. "I'm sorry."

Christian ignored the pleas and began to beat David within an inch of his life. He kicked and punched repeatedly, targeting the raw portions of David's wounds. David would swear that Blackheart watched from above, but couldn't tell whether it was him or a shadow.

Blackheart was in actuality observing the beating, hoping it would engage David further, using Christian as the bait.

Christian dragged David by the leg to a tree and used the rope to tie him down. David tried to cut the rope with his nails, but Christian overpowered each arm, slamming them down onto jagged extensions of the tree, puncturing each palm, leaving David crucified.

David cried out in excruciating pain and continued to plead with Christian, who now grabbed his ax. Christian sensed the fear and absorbed it, feeding his wrath. He picked up the ax overhead and as it was brought down, it was caught and stopped by Blackheart, who appeared on the scene at the last second. He stared at Christian, snapping the ax in half like a toothpick with one hand. Portraying a hero, Blackheart now hoped to regain David's trust.

"You've made your choice," Blackheart growled at Christian as his hounds appeared and chased Christian into his car.

He escaped without being harmed and sped off. The dogs ran back to their master, who threw David over his shoulder and walked him back to his dwelling.

"You need to drink, or you'll be dead within the hour," he told David.

Despite the lack of awareness, David uttered, "I deserve to die."

They reached the house, and the dogs brought various animals to David as Blackheart forced him to drink against his will to save his life. He squeezed all types of woodland animals dry, dripping blood into David's mouth. David struggled to drink it all and gagged, but Blackheart continued to feed him.

"Why won't you let me die?"

"Because you mean too much to me," he replied. "I lost Timothy. I won't lose you too."

David passed out, now understanding that whoever Timothy was, he no longer lived, but David was still unsure of the relationship to Blackheart.

Blackheart looked on, assured David's wounds would heal soon and he would recover in full. The blood was their life force. He sat beside David for the remainder of the night, caressing him like a concerned parent, as the dogs did the same.

27

Alliance

David sat in the back of the church with Alexandra, listening to Father Richard's service. They didn't speak at all to each other, but there was no awkwardness, and his anxiety had been silenced. He had been revived from Christian's attack and left Blackheart's company after several days. He didn't know who to trust now except Alex and Father Richard.

The service ended, and both of them went toward Father Richard's office. David told her all about Christian's attack and still sported some of the wounds he'd been dealt. Feeling an invigorated sense of empathy, she put her hand on one of the scars on David's neck and expressed deep concern. David was petrified of leaving the church again, as was she. There was no telling who or what was outside the walls of their current sanctuary.

"I don't want you to get hurt, David. I care too much about you," she said. "You've been through enough."

They both looked at one another, unsure of their feelings at this point. Alexandra grabbed his hand gently and led him to her father. David felt her soft skin and swooned. He felt extremely fulfilled with something as simple as one person who cared for him like this.

They then sat with Father Richard, who overheard some of their conversation en route to his office. He was pleased to see how his daughter had gotten past her judgmental habits and even developed a friendship with David.

He was positive that she would be able to run the church when he was no longer able to one day. She could be the spiritual guidance that his congregation, and the town, would so desperately need. Father Richard smiled at Alexandra. Her exposure to a situation like David's had opened his daughter's mind quite a bit and would teach her many valuable lessons that would benefit her in future instances.

They all sat together before David looked deep into Alex's eyes. Gentle warmth and clarity came over him, and he realized he must confront Blackheart. Despite all of his fears, anxiety, and everything trying to block him from doing so, he must try his best to stop anyone else from getting hurt. He left the company of his friends and made his way to Chrysanthemum Drive.

* * *

Across town, Christian awakened in a dark room, not at all aware of his location. He'd been kidnapped and knocked out by someone hours before.

As his vision cleared, he recognized the dining room in Blackheart's home, where he was seated at the one end of the large dinner table. A soft piano played, but he couldn't see the player. Candles were lit all around him. He tried to stand up, but Blackheart's hounds sat next to him, growling and staring him down.

"I wouldn't move much. They haven't been fed in some time," Blackheart said, revealing himself, lighting the remainder of the candles.

The additional light illuminated an unconscious man strapped to the dinner table in front of Christian.

"I can't say that I agree with your decision, but I understand it," Blackheart continued, going toward the opposite end of the table and sitting down.

He reached forward and pulled a toe off of the man, waking him up gruffly as he screamed through a mouth gag. Blackheart examined it, licking a bit of the blood off before throwing it to the dogs, who fought over it. Christian tried to move again, but they turned their attention to him, making him sit back down.

"Something very bad happened to me a very long time ago. Right here in this town. By the person they called Mr. Smith."

Blackheart wiped blood off the victim's foot and let it roll down his palm, enjoying the music as it set a disturbing tone for the already dreadful scene.

He pulled a piece of skin off the victim's thigh, again tossing it toward his dogs. It slapped the floorboard in a vile manner, sending blood onto the leg of the table next to Christian, who finally figured out that Blackheart had been a victim of Mr. Smith.

"Smith took you as a child." Christian shuddered.

"Indeed, he did. I vowed that I would make them pay for it. This town. All of them. They took no action. Just like with your daughter. Caroline, right? Has anything been done about it?"

Christian gripped the arms of his chair, becoming increasingly uncomfortable as the man strapped to the table wiggled and screamed.

"Each family here will continue to pay a penance to me. They deserve it. The rest will be spared. Every few generations, they all need to be reminded of the mistakes of their past family members," he said, revealing a distinct killing pattern of his victims.

Blackheart moved up to his victim's stomach, puncturing his abdomen, pulling out a handful of viscera.

"Your parents . . . Caroline . . . I don't want to harm your family any more than they already have been. You're all paid up. Well, for a while, that is. Your son's family one day. I'm afraid they'll be next up."

The dogs looked to Blackheart to drop the gore, which he made them beg for before slopping it on the ground.

"You and I are two in the same, Christian. We are both very angry at this place. But we stay here and enjoy the resentment. We're comfortable with it. We just stay on opposite sides of the spectrum, which is why we have issues with one another."

Blackheart put a hand over the man's mouth, further muffling his struggle. "But you stay and now come after me and my attempt at a family? Almost repeating the same injustice you suffered yourself? For your own ego? At the sake of your wife and son?"

"That boy is not your family. He's just your next victim," Christian growled.

Christian tried to slide off his chair, but one of the dogs ran to his side and monitored him closely as the others continued to dine.

"Christian, I really don't want to hurt you. I am very comfortable with tradition, but you're not giving me any choice."

He opened more of the man's stomach and started throwing organs at Christian's face, walking up to him as the dogs picked up everything that hit the floor. The victim stopped moving, and the music ended.

"You can't stop this. The way this all works. It's my town. They make money and sit comfortably because I allow them to do so off of my name. And they, in return, allow me to uphold my traditions here. The town and I complement each other. We need one another. We want each other. We are one. And you don't stand a chance against us." He got face-to-face with Christian. "So all you need to do is go away and never come back. I can't be any more merciful than this."

Christian didn't accept Blackheart's ultimatum. He spat blood into Blackheart's face. He snarled and grabbed Christian, who tried to push him off but couldn't match his strength.

"You're not worth this kind of effort. The dogs can have you," he said as the three hounds looked up, dripping blood and saliva from the sides of their distended mouths.

"You have no bite marks," Christian uttered, noticing no apparent marks on Blackheart's neck.

Blackheart let go and gave him a puzzled look.

"You were never bitten, were you?" Christian began to tease. "You were turned another way by Smith."

Blackheart now sported a very pained look and backed up.

"You were raped. All those allegations about Smith were true," Christian concluded, watching Blackheart become more human, showing vulnerability.

"He hurt me very badly. For years and years and years. This town let it go on. And God let it happen. And do you know what someone in that situation has to do when they're abandoned by their God?"

"No," Christian said, completely scared of the conclusion of this conversation.

"They must become one themselves. They must rule as they see fit. I am now God in this town," he said in a very stoic, narcissistic way.

Blackheart flipped the table over, and the dogs backed off, scared. He went behind Christian, holding him down, and the dogs began to lick his boots.

"I admire how smart and spirited you are. I'm going to enjoy watching this." The dogs now began eating the pant legs off of Christian, licking his legs with their very rough tongues, taking some skin off.

Christian prayed that something would save him, and David walked through the front door.

"What the hell are you doing?" David asked Blackheart.

Blackheart seemed unsure of his excitement with David returning again.

"I'm doing what's necessary. Now go back to church with your little friends. We'll deal with them soon enough."

"You're not going to hurt them. I can't let you hurt him. He's lost enough," David said, now seeing the extent of Blackheart's ugliness. David relinquished any anger he had for Christian and directed it toward his former mentor.

Blackheart sneered at David, beginning to view him as a failed experiment. The inability to kill, lack of appreciation for Blackheart's efforts, abandoning him to spend time with Father Richard and Alexandra, and now challenging his decisions had all dissuaded Blackheart from continuing on with his protégé.

"So this is how it goes? If that's how you feel, then you join the ranks of those people out there," he directed at David.

In the blink of an eye, David grabbed Christian and crashed through the wall nearest to them to escape the house. They bounded across the wooded area, hearing the hounds follow. Christian slid through some dirt patches and narrowly avoided being bitten several times. They reached Highway 6 and jumped into the road, using the speeding cars as distractions to continue avoiding the dogs. The drivers screeched and skidded all around the bunch, causing several accidents. David and Christian were separated but managed to continue avoiding the predators on their own. One of the hounds closed in on David, but the loud sound of Blackheart's violin reached them, and the dogs retreated. David collected himself and he looked for his partner, but Christian had already run off.

28

Acceptance

Police Chief Jones sat on a phone call with Mayor Wilkins.

"Jones, you're getting so sloppy. Do you realize how many calls I'm getting every day about all these missing persons, sightings, and all?"

"Mayor, I have all the police tours being advised on how to handle. We're all working overtime and can't do any more than we're already doing. The creature is more active in the last few months than ever before. We've seen more than one of them now too. It's just getting too hard to keep all this covered up."

"This is an election year. I can't have any of this bad press. Update your advanced directives for your men and do whatever the hell you need to fix this. And I want two more officers at town hall when I'm in my office. You wouldn't believe how

many of these crazy people are coming here to threaten me
and make a scene."

"Yes, ma'am. Understood."

"Because if I lose this election, you'll be out too. Remember
that," she barked, slamming the phone down.

Chief Jones poured a tall glass of whiskey and drank half
of it without taking a breath. He thought back to the look on
Christian Reed's face when his officers hauled him away and
felt a deep sense of guilt.

"The problem and the solution," he muttered at the alcohol, feeling exasperated with the situation he'd been aware of
for several decades on the police force.

His wife, Martha, walked into the room, hearing the end
of the conversation, and put her hands on hips to get his attention. "What are you doing?"

"I've gotten too old for this," he said, almost despondent.

"It's just been a messy patch lately. It's happened before,
and it always slows down. You've been doing this long enough
to know that," she assured him.

"Not like this. We've got dozens dead. Kids in there. It just
takes one reporter to go against the grain and start telling the
truth, and this town is screwed. We're all screwed."

"You say that like anyone would believe it. This town is so
big. Everyone here knows how this all works. We accept it for
what it is and the risks of living here. When you look at how
many people live here without incident versus those who do,
it's so minimal. It's no more dangerous than any other place to
live. It's a perfect town beyond this one issue. We don't have

earthquakes or any natural disasters. Just this one atypical thing here. If we continue to appease it, it leaves us alone." Martha tried to justify the traditions of Meadowsville and soothe her husband.

"I need to retire," he said. "We need to move. I'm starting to crack up here. It's too much."

"Our entire family is here. All of our friends. It wouldn't make sense," she replied.

Chief Jones drank the rest of his beverage and almost passed out sitting upright.

"Come on, let's get you to bed."

His wife helped him stand up, and they went to their bedroom for the night. They never resumed the conversation.

Chief Jones knew that Mayor Wilkins would not get reelected this time. Things had become too unhinged. He had to decide whether to risk being part of any eventual investigation or salvage what was left of his career and finally try to make things right.

29

Destruction

Blackheart sat in his house, looking at the now rotting victim on his destroyed dinner table, languishing in the odor of stinking flesh. He breathed it in deeply and began to lose control. He had had past Meadowsville residents attempt to come after him, but none like Christian. He had truly figured out Blackheart better than anyone else in the town's history. This made Blackheart uneasy.

He had had dozens of students prior to David but none with more potential. Losing David after all his efforts, over a decade, was unacceptable. He would force Christian and David out of hiding to finally put them down like disobedient animals. He would destroy the town, however necessary, to achieve it. The traditions he had relied on would now be disregarded. This was Meadowsville and would remain his town forever.

"It begins," he said to his hounds as he plotted his treacheries.

He transformed and entered Meadowsville in clear view that night, no longer keeping to the shadows. He heard an angelic violin song in his head as he reigned down a spree of devastation onto the town.

He entered a four-way stop and was almost run over by one of the town tour buses, but he shoved it over, injuring everyone inside it. Soon after, a roaming posse of teenagers saw him. They stupidly dropped their weapons and started snapping pictures, celebrating their accomplishment. He and the three dogs ripped the group into pieces within seconds, licking the blood off the street, all killing like a pack.

A police car arrived, not seeing Blackheart on the ground eating one of the victims. It screeched to a halt as he lifted his head. Blackheart stood tall and delivered a single blow to the hood, smashing the entire front of the car and starting a fire. He and the dogs roared into the night so loudly that all of the nearby windows rattled. The officer crawled out of the car and fired wildly, missing Blackheart with every shot, and ran off, calling for backup. Several more neighborhood watch groups and gangs quickly arrived on the scene and saw Blackheart and his dogs. They all began attacking him as a group, but he knocked them off one by one, laughing at their efforts. There was now no more mystery of the creature that had ruled over Meadowsville all these years. The town could no longer cover up all the atrocities Blackheart had committed. The game had changed forever now.

Blackheart and the dogs slaughter several of the groups' members as the others started to retreat. Blackheart waited for more cop cars and first responders to arrive on scene. As they did, the hounds bit through the tires and sent the cars crashing into the nearby businesses, starting fires all around them.

Blackheart took one of the officers who was still alive and proceeded to walk to the town hall, dragging him like a caveman. More citizens saw him in person for the first time as he walked casually through the streets, surrounded by the dogs, and ran for their lives. The chaos spread quickly across the town. All of the gangs, police, and willing citizens banded together and vowed to kill the creature once and for all. The time for a revolution in Meadowsville had begun.

He approached the town hall and lifted the officer into the air, roaring up toward the mayor's office on the second floor. He pulled the officer's arms off, then his legs, and finally his head. The pieces of the officer flopped into a bloody pile of mush and stained the steps of the town hall. Mayor Wilkins looked on, truly fearful for the first time in her long political career. She realized how far out of control she'd let things get. Her phone rang, and she saw it was Police Chief Jones's number, but she didn't answer. She knew deep down that he was coming to arrest her and that everything would be exposed. She sat at her desk, hearing the town destroy itself, and prepared for what was about to come to her.

Blackheart was distracted as he smelled Alexandra nearby, remembering her unique scent from the church. He leapt several blocks away, leaving hordes of rioting citizens behind as they pursued him. The town was no longer divided but rather united against the common threats now. The fires spread, and the normal nightlife in Meadowsville was now overtaken with sirens, screaming, and explosions.

Blackheart leapt higher than ever before, coasting down toward Alexandra. She was on her way home, late for curfew and unaware of the current state of the town. He landed next to her at a traffic light. She didn't notice him until he pulled the driver-side door off with ease. She crawled over the console into the passenger side seat, trying to get out. Blackheart got in and leaned over, almost on top of her. Her silver Ford Focus tilted toward the side Blackheart sat, due to his immense volume.

"If you get out, I'll catch you before your foot hits the ground."

She sat in place, terrified, as Blackheart fiddled with the radio, eventually finding a station airing only romantic music and blared it to the point of hurting Alexandra's ears. He sped off, going over a hundred miles per hour, crashing into other cars and some of the rebelling townspeople, rousing the remainder of the town. Alexandra bore witness to the destruction of Meadowsville and hoped that the police would save her, but they were all preoccupied with managing the rioting citizens and ravaging of the town. They passed under several streetlights, onward to an unknown destination. Each light revealed an increasingly hideous Blackheart as he devolved into something worse than ever before.

He stopped the car at the entrance of Meadowsville Community Church and looked at Alexandra with a dragon-like face. He hit the radio again as a very animated love song came on.

I need your love
To comfort my soul

"I want you to run. Run for your life. Because if I get you . . . I'm gonna hurt you really bad. So bad that you'll be in pain even in death," Blackheart said in a surprisingly controlled manner, demonstrating full control over his powers.

Just try to trust me
And give it time

She opened the door and sprinted toward the building, yelling for help. Blackheart sat inside and breathed deeply, enjoying the calm before he attacked. Alexandra screamed for her father. Blackheart opened his eyes wide, leapt out of the car, and landed on her. She struggled, but he held her down, admiring her straight black hair becoming messy.

"You're as close to God as I can get," he said putting his dirty hand across her hair, pulling some of it out.

Another car sped into the parking lot and Christian ran into Blackheart, distracting him, allowing Alexandra to roll out of the way. Christian got out and helped Alex run inside as Blackheart stood up, ready to pounce. As he did, David unexpectedly tackled him from the side. The two wrestled each other, and Christian joined in, trying to stab Blackheart with a knife he had in his pocket. Blackheart managed to overpower both, and the three men neared the front doors of the church. Alexandra reemerged and struck Blackheart from behind with a vase full of holy water. He had an immediate reaction as part of the skin melted off his face. He roared, jumping into the night.

The three individuals stared at one another. Alexandra took both their hands, before either man could do anything, and joined them, repelling their individual resistance to do so. This was her first time being assertive and entering into a leadership role. Her meekness began to diminish.

"None of us can do this without the others," she said, acting as the voice of reason. "You both know that. We have to stop him."

Christian resisted the urge to attack David but understood the situation and need for his help. David, knowing the full extent of Blackheart's power and abilities, knew that he needed help too.

"This doesn't change anything between us," Christian said to David, completely negating the fact he was saved by this young man very recently.

David nodded, and the three went into the church.

30

Preparation

Hours later, David returned to Meadowsville Community Church with stolen equipment from the police building. He'd witnessed absolute anarchy in the town. At the town hall, the mayor's office was being burned down, and she was in hiding in an undisclosed location. The police were out in full force but were no match for the sheer volume of what was happening. With their department empty aside from dispatchers, David was able to sneak in and get to their equipment storage room to search for any type of armor for Christian.

David dropped down riot gear, various weapons, and personal protective equipment as Christian pieced things together without thanking David.

"We know that holy water and regular attacks hurt him," Christian said.

"Only if we believe something will hurt us, will it actually do so," David chimed in.

"Blackheart is afraid of the church. We know that now. Any type of weaponry we can make from the church will be of use," Alex added.

Christian soaked some of the gloves in holy water and put them on, along with brass knuckles on one hand. Alexandra helped him put on a bulletproof vest, joint pads, a loaded tool belt, and heavy-duty work boots that had the steel toes exposed. Christian noticed a new ax in the pile, which he grabbed with some sense of entitlement. He was ready to go to war.

"You remind me of my daughter," he said to Alexandra, becoming sentimental. "We lost her recently to all this."

Alex nodded with empathy.

"I wasn't able to protect her, but I promise that you'll get out of this safely," he declared to her.

He grabbed her unexpectedly and hugged her, struggling with his emotions, being on the brink of a personal breakthrough. She accepted the hug then nervously assembled her own protective equipment, which wasn't much more than some protective padding and a knife that she also dipped into holy water, hiding it in her back pocket.

"Service is starting," David said referring to Father Richard's one late weeknight church service going on in the main portion of the church.

A small crowd of scared Meadowsville residents attended, praying for some semblance of stability in the town that night.

"Do we go after him now or wait?" Christian asked.

"No, he'll be back for us," David confirmed.

The three of them sat behind the scenes to hear Father Richard begin his sermon. Unlike his normal sermons, this was very heated and direct. Because it had to be . . .

"God gives us the ability to have faith in Him. Some listen, hear His word, and base their lives on it, whereas others choose not to. They choose to become their own gods. Disobeying His rules and making up their own guide to living, silencing what their souls are screaming out to them."

Christian peeked out to see a large crowd, all visibly uneasy due to the mayhem in town.

"Then the lines between what is just and what is not become blurred. Nothing is held sacred at that point. Not life, not your fellow man, not God, nothing of importance. Just superficial nonsense like money and ego. It leads us into a time of acceptable sin and injustice. Every person for themselves and whatever their agendas are. No accountability or remorse. And all of His people engage in total anarchy, against His wishes, as we see in Meadowsville tonight."

Blackheart stood outside one of the windows, staring right at Christian. He went back to Alexandra and David and warned them of Blackheart's presence.

"But . . . God stays true to all, despite their poor choices. Despite their hate toward one another, rejection of Him, and all of their sins, He remains loyal. Not judging but understanding and loving. And we must all remember that. We are all the same in his eyes. Not even the most wicked of us are beyond his reach. God will always bring us together in the end," Father Richard finished.

Blackheart walked away as Father Richard made the last statement. Blackheart left without issue, taunting Christian, David, and Alexandra.

31

Origin

Many years ago in Meadowsville, a young boy sat alone in a cement cellar, with a small radio playing in the corner. He was huddled across from it, seemingly starved and beaten, and all he had to pass the time was the music that played.

He strongly resembled David at the same age.

The large door was unlocked and an older man with a distorted face peeked in. This was John Smith.

"Timothy, please come out here," he asked, putting his hand out to the boy.

The boy quickly walked out into the next room and saw a man lying on the floor crying.

"You have to get comfortable with this," Smith said, biting the man's neck and drinking the blood that poured out.

Timothy closed his eyes hard, focusing on the sound of the music instead of the attack, but Smith pulled him forward and forced him to partake. He flinched as the old man touched him, and he felt the pain in his mouth from his teeth extending out.

Timothy lifted his head from the bloody corpse, fighting back tears. "Please let me go, Mr. Smith," he begged. "My parents miss me. They'll come looking for me. I won't tell anyone what you did to me. I swear."

The old man laughed hard, showing no signs of compassion. "Oh, my boy, your parents are dead. And the town stopped the search for you."

Timothy started to tear up.

"Don't cry. You remember what happens when you cry in front of me," Smith said.

Timothy backed up quickly, protecting his backside against the wall, afraid of yet another sexual assault by this truly evil individual.

"Don't worry. I could never bite you. Your skin is just too perfect."

Mr. Smith picked up his violin and began to play, making Timothy stand there and listen as the victim's body lay still before them both. Timothy asked himself where God was but received no answer, much like David would one day do.

"At least your playing has improved. We'll work on the rest," Smith said to Timothy, as he had taught him to play little bits of music over the previous few weeks.

This abuse went on for many years as Timothy became acclimated to killing and living as a monster, using music as an eventual aphrodisiac. As he became older, he plotted to kill Mr. Smith, who ended up dying of old age before Timothy was able to see his plan through. Smith was buried deep beneath the soil under his house on Chrysanthemum Drive, polluting the earth with his tainted blood. Blackheart made sure a memorial gravestone was placed in town to honor him.

It was at this point that Timothy took over the mantle of Mr. Smith, using his own unique persona to terrorize Meadowsville, giving himself the name Blackheart. His sole ambition was to make the town pay for what was done to him, all while satisfying his animalistic urges. He kept Mr. Smith's violin, remained in his residence, and continued his legacy, paying homage to his mentor. As he began his reign over Meadowsville, the rare news reports of killings being perpetrated by someone with a *cold, black heart* were adopted as his own persona.

32

War

Alex, Christian, and David waited in the church for many hours into the night, eagerly anticipating Blackheart's next move, praying with Father Richard after the service concluded. Suddenly, a violin permeated the building, interrupting the conclusion of their prayer and announcing that Blackheart was ready for them outside. Father Richard asked Alexandra not to join the men, but she insisted, making her own decisions for the first time in her young life. Against her father's wishes, she chose to go outside into the cemetery with them. Father Richard blessed the three of them, taking extra time with David, acknowledging that he needed the most support from God in this horrible situation.

"I'm coming with you," Father Richard said to the group, readying himself.

Christian and David both looked at Alexandra, who walked to her father and looked deep into his eyes, almost penetrating his soul.

"Dad, I know you want to be there. You've always been such a strong role model. But I need to do with alone." Alexandra cemented her growth.

Proud of his daughter's quick development in the past few weeks, he respected her wishes and gave her a hug.

"I've never been more proud of you," he said with glassy eyes.

He always felt that with the loss of his wife, he had perhaps been too strict and controlling of his daughter. But all of his fears were now laid to rest. His baby girl was ready to begin her journey into adulthood and beyond.

The three went out into the graveyard and saw Blackheart standing in the center of it, surrounded by his hounds. As they neared, he played what might be his final ballad, continuing with his eyes closed. He suddenly made a mistake and stopped playing. He opened his eyes abruptly and smashed the instrument against a nearby gravestone that read, *John Smith*. Blackheart morphed into the most hideous version of horror that could be seen. A new form that would send fear into the most courageous soul.

"David, you were being groomed to take over for me one day. You were supposed to be like a God to these insects. Now you're undeserving of the honor. You and your friends will die like all the others who have stood in my way. I am the black heart of this town, and that will never change," he proclaimed.

The sounds of rioting citizens were heard as they spread through the remainder of the town. Christian and David stood in front of Alex, who now held her one knife, still dripping in holy water, that she concealed earlier. Blackheart began to hear a guitar cover of a sonata in his mind as he prepared for battle, and his plunge into total insanity concluded.

"Take them," he commanded his dogs. They obeyed and flanked their three aggressors.

David threw Alexandra up into a nearby tree, as she didn't have much to protect herself with. One dog chased her and barked at the base, trying to climb up. Another bit David's arm and dragged him to Blackheart as Christian ran from the third.

Christian grabbed a screwdriver from his belt and slid along the damp grass between graves, puncturing the eye of his accompanied dog as it closed in on him. It howled in pain and swung its head around, trying desperately to dislodge the tool.

"David!" Alexandra yelled, seeing him being mauled, bringing Blackheart's attention to her.

David was brought to Blackheart's feet, who grabbed his leg, smashing him through a large gravestone. David spit up blood and looked to Alexandra, who was stuck in the tree. Blackheart walked over to her, still enjoying the music in his mind. David tried to get up but stumbled down repeatedly from the pain. The one dog continued its assault on him, biting into his thigh, down to the bone.

Christian grabbed the ax on his back and hacked at the injured dog, killing it. As he was pulling the ax out, the second dog left David and tackled Christian. It bit his armored chest plate, whipping him frantically and slamming him onto the ground. David stirred and jumped to Christian's aide, pulling off the animal's lower jaw, with the entire anterior portion of its body coming with it. David licked his hand to keep blood in his system and maintain his strength. Christian nodded in thanks.

Alexandra lowered herself as the last hound left but then saw Blackheart below. He pushed the tree and knocked it over, sending her crashing to the ground. He loomed over Alexandra, exposing his teeth fully, bobbing his head slightly to the music continuing to play in his thoughts. More of his skin dripped off from her earlier attack on him with the holy water in the church parking lot.

David was bitten by the final hound as it tore at his already injured leg. Christian grabbed it from the side, flipping it backward onto a tombstone and injuring its back. The animal didn't release its grip on David until both men pulled down from opposite ends, almost breaking it in half and finally killing it.

Both men collected themselves and ran to Blackheart, who had Alexandra in his hands as she fended off his attempt to bite her neck. He roared and pulled her closer, but Alex stabbed him in the shoulder with her knife. She was the first person to ever injure Blackheart, and that scared the creature to the bottom of its core. It also brought Alexandra out of a certain level of innocence that she had always lived in.

Blackheart threw her as he began to hemorrhage, but David caught her. Christian was leveled with a devastating punch as Blackheart flailed his arms, trying to get the knife out. Alex got away from David, ran up, and pulled the knife down along Blackheart's arm, disabling him even more. He attempted to strike her, but David took the hit, knocking her out of the way. A small beam of sunshine came through the sky as daylight began to come onto the scene. Blackheart tried to flee, but David grabbed his coat, holding him back.

"He is weakened with the sunlight. Keep him here," David yelled to his comrades.

Christian jumped on Blackheart's back, holding him tightly as he kicked David into another gravestone, breaking it in half. David was momentarily stymied and looked to find Alex. They comforted each other briefly.

Unable to dislodge Christian, Blackheart retreated to his mansion with tremendous leaps. Christian held on for dear life, pulling the knife lodged in Blackheart's arm in every direction to hurt him further. They landed in the mansion, crashing through the roof. Christian and Blackheart fell apart, both hurt. An angry mob was already outside the home, setting fire to it, exposing their weapons and yelling, "Death to Smith!"

Blackheart roared at his onlookers through the open doors as they scurried away from the battle. Christian sidelined him with several hard punches, using the brass knuckles and holy water–soaked gloves to damage him greatly. As Blackheart lowered to one knee, weakened, Christian began kicking him with his steel-toe boots, debilitating him almost completely. Christian had flashbacks of his parents, and Caroline, as he landed more devastating hits. Christian wouldn't stop himself. He refused to.

Blackheart managed to punch Christian directly in the chest guard, shattering it, knocking him into a nearby wall. Blackheart looked around as his home burned and didn't care anymore that the town had unanimously revolted against him. He began to feel closer to death than ever before, and he was afraid. He couldn't focus as he moved like an injured animal, making horrific sounds of desperation.

David finally arrived, using his incredible speed to make it to the location quickly, slashing at Blackheart's neck and torso and cutting off his signature coat, exposing an overly muscular and vascular figure marred by thousands of scars. He grabbed David by the head and slammed him into the floor, breaking several boards.

The music in Blackheart's mind turned to static as Christian took a flaming piece of wood and stabbed him from behind. Christian held his position, pushing the weapon through the front of Blackheart's body, watching him struggle. David recovered and grabbed the other side of the wood as they worked as a team to lift Blackheart into the air. Blackheart cried out in extreme agony and managed to terminally slash David across the neck. All three men fell to the ground, exhausted and incapacitated.

Christian crawled to an injured David, who apologized for the pain he put Christian through.

"I'm so sorry for hurting you," David said, and blood poured from his mouth with each word. "I know you don't believe me, but I am. I never meant to hurt anyone."

For the first time in his life, Christian accepted the words and their sincerity as he finally learned what it meant to forgive.

He now saw the fear in David's eyes. He became sentimental. He remembered the fear and uncertainty he had when he was David's age, having no parents, no guidance, and no hope. He now fully understood that David was just a scared young boy, not a malicious beast.

"I'm sorry too. I'm sorry I couldn't save you like my daughter," he said, tearing up at the personal epiphany. This was also the first time he had issued a genuine apology in his life.

David thought of his parents, Erik, and finally the kiss he surprised Alexandra with in the cemetery before pursuing Blackheart and Christian earlier.

"You were the best thing to ever happen to me," he had told Alexandra before leaving her, their matching emerald eyes locking for possibly the last time.

He now realized that God had been present all along and both Alexandra and Father Richard were clear signs of that. He had never been forgotten.

"I have been saved . . ." David said to Christian, dying in the next instant.

Blackheart twitched on the ground, coughing up blood as Christian used his last bit of energy to crawl over to him. They lay next to each other, watching carefully as the house fell apart from the flames all around them. Blackheart tried to talk but was too injured to put together any words coherently. Christian also felt empathy for Blackheart, who was just a misguided, tortured soul.

"I understand your pain. Your anger. All of it. And you were right. We weren't much different from each other. But no longer. Things need to change. I need to change. And this town no longer needs you," he said, taking off his holy cross and placing it into Blackheart's hands, putting it against his chest.

Blackheart closed his eyes and seemingly passed away peacefully, holding the cross tightly. It did not burn or hurt him, meaning upon his death, he might have finally been cured of his fear of God. The house continued to collapse, falling on top of Blackheart's body, pushing it deep into the soil beneath the foundation.

Christian stood up and exited the still burning inferno, holding onto everything near him to not fall. They all lowered their rakes, shovels, guns, and other weapons and looked to Christian with a renewed faith. He had killed the legend that this town was built around. He had given them a fresh start.

"It's over," Christian declared in a mighty tone. "It's finally over."

He stood for several more seconds before collapsing from his exhaustion and sustained injuries. The other residents rushed to collect Christian as he fell and pulled him away from the house. They all remained in front of the house, watching until there were nothing left but smoldering embers, before leaving with their hero.

33

Transition

Weeks later, Father Richard, Alexandra, Christian, Rebecca, and Adam stood at Caroline's grave. Christian was still bandaged up from the injuries he acquired battling Blackheart, but he maintained himself with great pride. He and Rebecca had found better ways to work with one another and now planned to work as a team to raise Adam in a better household than before.

Father Richard spoke kind, warm words for the losses they had all endured during the recent times. Rebecca pulled Alexandra in close, hugging her, giving her the mother figure she'd desired since losing her own. The day was picture perfect, and all was calm in Meadowsville for the unorthodox family unit.

As the prayers concluded, they all walked away, but Alexandra and Christian saw David's memorial gravestone. She shed a single tear and smiled up at the sky as Christian gave her a gentle nod of respect as they walked toward the church. They neared the building and admired a powerful nearby American flag flying strong in the breeze. As the flag remained steadfast, echoing a revived and rehabilitated town, a loose piece of newspaper stuck to the side of the church that read, *Massive Conspiracy in Meadowsville. Mayor Wilkins Arrested by Police Chief Jones.*

Everyone entered the church, but Christian stayed outside with Adam, holding him up toward the bright sun, assuring his son that Meadowsville was different now.

Or was it?

To be continued . . .

Thank you so much for reading my debut novel. I hope you enjoyed the first entry in the Preternatural trilogy. I would greatly appreciate it if you could consider writing a review on Amazon and/or Goodreads.

I love to connect with readers, so please feel also free to reach out directly and follow me on Instagram @Ptopside, Twitter @PTopside, Facebook @topsidepeter, and Bookbub.

And please check out the next installment in the trilogy, *Preternatural: Evolution*. Turn the page for a sneak peek . . .

Alex now felt the sensation grow, resembling a migraine, but it was more unique, which caused her to end her sermon prematurely.

"Let us pray . . ." When everyone bowed their heads, she continued. "Lord God, thank You for sacrificing Your only son for our sinful ways. We confess it all to You to renew us."

The sensation became stronger, but she tried to push past it. She felt Blackheart's presence somehow, as if he were standing in front of her. He was there with her. She was so sure of it.

"When sin and evil work against us, we remain steadfast and true to You. We trust that Your word is the only word, and You will guide us in the most righteous way. Give us Your light and give us the chance to be reflections of Your peace during a time when this world needs Your presence and healing. Help give us the strength to help those who experience hard times, pain, death, and other worldly misfortunes. Be with us as we rejoice in Your triumphs."

She felt off balance and stumbled but steadied herself on the pulpit. Several members got out of their seats to help her but stopped when she caught herself. In her mind, Alexandra saw Blackheart's mansion in its present form, and she felt his power surge.

"Whoever believes in You will be given new life," she said, now seeing Blackheart's burnt hand crash out of the debris on Chrysanthemum Drive.

In that moment, the connection to him was fully forged. He had gotten into her mind and used her to give himself enough strength to come back.

She crashed to the floor of the altar.

About the Author

PETER TOPSIDE is an author, reviewer, and horror fanatic. He is also an accomplished chef and baker; a prouder father and husband; and a Clinical Exercise Physiologist by trade.